Where Do They All Belong?

THE POTTER'S HOUSE BOOKS TWO – BOOK 15

CHLOE S. FLANAGAN

NOTE FROM THE AUTHOR

The 24 books that form The Potter's House Books Series Two are linked by the theme of hope, redemption, and second chances. They are all stand-alone books and can be read in any order. Books will become progressively available from January 7, 2020.

Book 9: *When Love Abounds*, by Juliette Duncan

Book 10: *More Than This*, Kristen M. Fraser

Book 11: *Faith's Favor*, by Mary Manners

Book 12: *Song of Mercy*, by Brenda S Anderson

Book 13: *In Spite of Ourselves*, by Jen Rodewald

Book 14: *Her Christmas Cowboy*, by Dora Hiers

Book 15: *Where Do They All Belong?* by Chloe Flanagan

Books 16: *Radiant Rays of Grace*, by Delia Latham

Books 17-24 to be advised

1

"You've been running for years, maybe your whole life."

Darla was strolling across the large church hall, but she froze at the sharp accusation.

"Do you think the facts will change if you ignore them? Grow up!"

Darla surprised herself by flinching. Natalie didn't face her directly, but she had the ability to command attention with her voice, making her words seep down into the soul and settle there. And she wasn't done. With a shake of her fist, she said, "You can't forget about the past forever!"

Darla cleared her throat. "Well, it's worth a try, isn't it?"

Natalie whirled around, noticing Darla's presence for the first time, and her face melted into a friendly smile. "Darla! How long have you been here?"

"Not long enough to see the whole scene, I'm afraid. Is this for a new role?"

"Yes. We haven't even started rehearsals yet, but I want to get some of the script worked out in my head before we do." Natalie gestured around the large fellowship hall. "This is a great place to practice while I wait for the kids to get here. The acoustics are phenomenal." A frown contorted her pretty face. "Did you think I sounded too melodramatic?"

Darla scoffed. "Does a big-time New York City stage star really need my input?"

"No one asks your opinion unless they want honesty, Darla,"

1

Natalie assured her with a grin.

Darla nodded and stroked her chin. "Hmm. Okay, then. I only heard a few lines, mind you. But they were quite intense."

"Intense in a good way?" Natalie held a hand over her heart. "Or intense in a Joan Crawford wannabe kind of way? You didn't like it, did you? Is that it? Darla, I still can't read you half the time! Was it too much?"

Darla let her agonize for a few more seconds, then leaned forward. "Intense in a compelling way. Honestly, you have such a gift for pulling the audience in immediately. I don't know how you do that."

"Oh, Darla, thank you!" Natalie squealed, rushing forward to plant a sloppy kiss on each cheek. "That makes my day."

"Take it easy, woman," Darla cringed. "It's not like I'm a theater critic or anything."

Natalie laughed and squeezed her shoulders. "No, you're much more important."

Darla raised a single eyebrow, prompting Natalie to shrug. "More important to me, anyway."

"Thank you, dear. You're just odd enough to probably mean that."

"Oh, how I love your backhanded compliments! That'll give me just the energy boost I need to finish setting up this snack bar."

As if the words "snack bar" were one of Pavlov's bells, a pack of teenagers and preteens appeared at the fellowship hall door and clamored inside.

Affectionate warmth pumped through Darla's heart as it always did when she saw the kids, though she couldn't help but grimace at the sudden cacophony of screeching sneakers and raised voices. Frankly, the acoustics in the hall were a little *too* phenomenal sometimes.

2

Clifton stared, unblinking, at the small silver-framed photograph until his cellphone alarm started to jingle, making him jump.

He reached down into his pocket to silence the alarm, then set the frame back down on the sofa table with a shudder. How long had he been standing there, trying to feel something? Anything.

He backed away from the table and turned to cross the living room's large Persian rug. But before he left the room, he cast another long glance at the photograph.

Lucinda had insisted on them posing for it at the last Fourth of July picnic in the park. He wasn't much for Kodak moments, but he'd agreed since it had seemed so important to her. He'd stood with his arm hung loosely around her shoulders and sent a begrudging grin to the camera. He hadn't been looking his best that day. The thick silver hair he prided himself in keeping neatly combed and trim was matted down thanks to the hot and humid summer day. Lucinda, on the other hand, had managed to still look clean, refreshed, and happy. The smile she'd flashed at the camera was so broad it was almost like she'd been laughing.

There, that should've made him feel something. Tenderness? Melancholy? Even shock that a single year, including the last two months spent fighting cancer, had so altered Lucinda's appearance that she scarcely looked like the same woman now.

But none of those emotions registered. There was nothing inside but the numbness that had held him captive for longer than he cared to admit.

Turning again, he shuffled down the hall and into Lucinda's room, where she had dozed off with her hospital bed set in a half upright position.

Crossing to the window, he pulled back the curtain even though it was already partway open. Lucinda always wanted lots of sunlight for the various plants and flowers her bridge club friends kept sending her. They dotted her night table and dresser, making the air thick with fragrance. Of course, Lucinda didn't have much of a sense of smell anymore.

As the sunlight trickled in, Lucinda stirred and opened her eyes, sending him a drowsy half grin.

"I'm sorry to wake you, Lu, but it's time for your meds."

"Mmm. You're so sweet." She turned to the window as if scanning the sky outside but without really focusing. "You've done so much: taking time from work, practically giving up your life, just to take care of me. That kind of devotion doesn't come along every day." Her gaze returned to him. "It doesn't even matter to me anymore, you know."

He looked up from her night table where he'd been sorting pills. "What doesn't?"

The corners of her mouth drifted up. "That you don't love me."

His fingers slipped and fumbled, upsetting two bottles. "Don't say that." He sat down on the bed. "What we have is—"

"No, it's okay. I'm not trying to pressure you." She pressed a shaky hand to his jaw. "But you deserve to be loved. And I'm going to help you."

"You don't need to worry about me."

Lucinda's expression turned cryptic. "I'm not worried. There's no need for worry when you have a plan. That's what Darla always says."

His jaw hardened at the mention of Darla's name. "Really? Is that what she says? And is that all she does when you two talk? Gives you a bunch of pithy sayings and hangs up? What about coming to visit you? She's your only sister for Pete's sake!"

"Shh. Easy," Lucinda soothed. "It doesn't matter. Besides, Darla's not the type of woman you push."

Forcing his face to relax, he leaned forward and kissed her forehead. "Okay, then. Whatever you say. I'll go make some tea."

But as he headed to the kitchen, the steel returned to his bones. *Not the type of woman you push. We'll see about that.*

3

Darla stood in the kitchen doorway after snack time and watched the kids collect their backpacks and the take-home bags she, Natalie, and Glenn had prepared for them.

When Father Reuben, her church's associate rector, had first asked her to help organize a youth group that would welcome kids from the least economically advantaged areas in the city, she would have never expected to still be involved almost two years later. Back then, she'd agreed to help—not because she knew the first thing about children, but because she wanted to help with a ministry, and her previous three attempts to do so had ended in what Father Reuben had charitably termed "personality clashes." Her fellow church members would've probably said that, rather than clashing, her personality had stampeded over theirs elephant-style, but that hadn't stopped Father Reuben from giving her another chance.

To her surprise, the boys and girls had quickly wiggled their way into her heart, invigorating her with their energy, humor, and even their more rebellious tendencies.

One by one, the kids began to file out of the fellowship hall, exchanging fist bumps or hugs with Glenn and Natalie as they left.

Darla couldn't help but snicker to think how three such unlikely people had ended up in charge of this group.

As a forty-something bachelor, Glenn had known even less about young people than she had, yet he'd volunteered to help with the youth group. His kind and easygoing temperament had quickly endeared him to both her and the kids.

Then there was Natalie.

Several months before, she'd been between acting roles and had agreed to help with the cooking for a summer camp. At first, she'd avoided the kids like they were all wearing poison ivy leis, but that had changed as the camp progressed. Now she was standing in a circle of giggling girls and comparing nail polish colors.

A tall, skinny boy jogged past Darla, pulling her from her thoughts. As soon as she recognized him, she shouted, "Carlo! Where do you think you're going?"

His shoes squeaked to a halt and he looked at her. "Whaddya mean?"

"Are you really gonna peace out without telling me what happened at school?"

"Oh. Right." A sheepish grin lit his brown eyes. "I went to the teacher and explained stuff just like you said."

"And?"

"And he said I could do some extra homework to bring up the grade."

Darla clapped her hands together once. "Ha! I thought so."

"Yeah, but how'd you know?"

She waved her hand. "Just wait till you get old, like me. You'll see there's not much you can't figure your way out of."

Glenn approached and slid his arm around Natalie's shoulders as they waved the kids off. "You ready for cleanup duty, sweetheart?"

"I think so. The—"

Darla's cellphone rang loudly and the couple turned toward the sound.

She pulled the phone from her jacket pocket and stepped away to answer it.

"This is Darla."

"Darla, it's Clifton."

Her teeth clacked shut and ground together. "Why do you have my number?"

He huffed in her ear noisily. "I've been with your sister for three years now, Darla. Why wouldn't I have it?"

She rolled her eyes. "Exactly! You've been *with* my sister for three years. Not married to her. Not even engaged. Three years and you're still a vague preposition."

"Please, spare me your judgments, Darla. At least I'm actually here. Why haven't you visited Lucinda yet?"

"I don't think my relationship with my sister is any of your concern."

"It *is* my concern if it breaks her heart. I don't know what hang-ups have kept you away all this time, but I don't see how anything could be so bad that you won't at least come and say goodbye to her."

A long shiver jolted through Darla's body and left goose bumps on her arms. "What?"

"Come on, Darla!" His voice grew even sterner. "We're talking advanced cancer here. It's been weeks since she stopped treatment, how long did you think she would last?"

Darla choked and held the phone away from her ear. Cancer? No, that couldn't be. Lucinda would have told her during one of their talks.

When Darla pulled the phone up again, Clifton was still talking, but her mind wouldn't focus on his words. Buzzing filled her ears until it drowned out his voice.

"Clifton, I have to go now," she stopped him mid-sentence. "Tell my sister I'll be in town soon."

She ended the call without waiting for a reply and stared at the phone's blank screen.

Suddenly, her arm dropped, causing the phone to slide to the ground. But she didn't bend down to pick it up. Instead, she sagged against the closest wall.

Lucinda couldn't be dying. She was the younger one.

"Darla?" A concerned voice called to her from across the room. "Darla, what's wrong?"

Glenn and Natalie hurried toward her. They were staring at her like they feared she was having a heart attack. She had to get a grip.

"That was Clifton." Darla managed to keep her voice steady.

Natalie sent Glenn a questioning glance.

"Clifton's her sister's boyfriend," he explained. Then he turned to Darla. "What'd he say? Did something happen to Lucinda?"

"Cancer. She doesn't have much time left, apparently."

They both gasped at her words, but Glenn spoke first. "Aw, Darla, that's awful. I'm so sorry."

She only nodded. "I—I have to go see her. I'm going home to book a flight and get ready."

Natalie rushed forward. "Do you need help?"

"No." Best keep her answers short. It was easier to keep from being shaky that way.

"And what about the trip?" Natalie continued. "Are you okay to go alone or would you like one of us to come with you?"

"No, why would I want that?" Darla snapped.

Natalie flinched and took a step back. "Okay. I'm sorry. Just let us know."

"I'm fine. I just need to get moving on these arrangements."

Darla bustled to the door and called, "Thanks" over her shoulder.

She stopped in the hallway for a moment to catch her breath.

Natalie's voice carried out after her. "I feel so bad for Darla. I hope I didn't make things harder by offering to help. The whole friendship thing is still new to me; I'm not very good at it."

"No, listen, sweetheart," Glenn said, "Darla can be hard to get close to. I mean, in all the time I've known her, I've never even seen her apartment."

"Oh, wow."

Darla scowled at the fellowship hall doorway. *What did that prove?*

After ruminating for a moment, she kept walking down the hall and out of the church.

4

Darla shut her apartment door and leaned against it, willing her tense back muscles to uncoil a bit so she could sit at her desk without cramping up like she had in the cab just now.

Placing her hands on her hips, she rocked from side to side and took in the space. Glenn's words drifted through her mind. "I've never even seen her apartment."

Even if he had, what would it tell him? The rugged brick walls and exposed pipes hanging above exuded the crisp, industrial feel she loved in an urban apartment, but it might seem austere to an outsider. If that didn't, then the sparse furnishings and decorations would. The dining room, living room, and her home office corner were all one continuous space, peppered with utilitarian metal frames for the table and desk and a beige, microfiber sofa with two coordinating, if rarely-occupied wingback chairs.

Shuffling to the center of the living room, she continued to ponder the area. A flat-screen TV and a few abstract paintings hung from the walls, but there were no photos. The only ones she really had were from the church youth group, but she kept those safely tucked away in a leather album on her bookshelf. The tall, sturdy case she'd had custom built also housed the dozens of books she'd collected, mostly in recent years, along with her collection of wildlife documentary DVDs. She'd always enjoyed playing them in the background during those long nights when she brought her work home.

A tiny shiver trickled through her as she took it all in. Not particularly welcoming, no. Maybe there was something about her whole life that was unwelcoming. Maybe that's what Glenn had really meant. Normal people invited friends into their homes. Friends showed up in times of stress . . . for normal people. People like Lucinda.

Her sister had always been kind, welcoming, and focused on community. Retirement hadn't changed that, either. If anything, she'd joined even more clubs and causes. No doubt, she had numerous friends surrounding her in her current crisis to help with doctor's appointments and to bring food or supplies.

A harsh guffaw escaped Darla's lips. A few of those friends were probably only too eager to extend that help to Clifton too. Tall, lean, impeccably dressed Clifton Peters with his thick silver hair and good humor would inevitably be a magnet to Lucinda's widow and divorcee friends as soon as the funeral was over.

Without the slightest warning, Darla's knees buckled and she sank onto the sofa behind her.

The funeral! How was this possible? Lucinda was the younger one! Had Clifton really been straight with Darla, or was he just being dramatic? Lucinda had looked perfectly fine just a little while ago.

Darla squeezed her eyes shut, furiously plundering her memories. When had that been? Easter? Christmas? Yes. Lucinda and Clifton had visited her in the city for Christmas . . . two and a half years ago.

She drew in a sharp breath. Had it been that long? Two and a half years since she'd spoken to her sister face to face. What was wrong with her? Her only family. Now she would see her again, but it would be to say goodbye.

Darla buried her head in her hands and groaned, a strangled, guttural sound almost unrecognizable as her own voice. But no tears came, just a throbbing pressure in her temples. Acute awareness of her solitude closed in around her. It had been her own doing, of course, from a lifetime of big and little choices all the way up to this evening, when she'd pushed Natalie away.

But as she sat for a while, face still in her hands, the pressure began to ease. Gradual serenity wrapped its way around her as a Scripture sprang to mind from a lesson she'd given the kids earlier.

She took a deep, fortifying breath. She may have chosen solitude more often than not but, thanks to God's grace, she wasn't completely alone.

5

Clifton's pencil scratched across the page in his sketchbook, forming strong, forceful lines and neat curves, but after a moment, he paused. The structure had a nice frame, but what now? With a growl, he made a giant X through the drawing. It was only a thought exercise, anyway. He hadn't designed so much as a toolshed since Lucinda had gotten worse and he'd taken time off from his architecture firm to look after her. Not that he'd been bursting with creative inspiration even then. He'd delivered on the projects he'd been hired to do, providing quality that seemed to satisfy his clients well enough, but the designs lacked that extra flair that used to distinguish his work.

That initial design process used to be a collaboration of mind, feeling, and even soul; for often as he worked, he had the sense that God had gifted him with that creative spark to make his projects come alive and seem special. But all of that had changed three years ago with one brief phone call from his ex-wife. After that, nothing had made sense anymore. God? Well, God was still God. But he wasn't up there pulling strings for Clifton anymore. And he wasn't there in the work anymore. Everything that came out of Clifton's brain seemed as illogical and inelegant as a random phone call.

Or a cancer diagnosis.

The noisy clash of the doorbell interrupted his thoughts, and he checked his watch. It was a little early for the mail. Pulling himself to his feet, he shook off the stiffness from sitting and headed out of the home office and down the hall. As he passed her room, he looked in on Lucinda and saw that she was reading.

As soon as he opened the front door, he took a step back. "Darla!"

"Clifton," she acknowledged him in a clipped tone.

Whatever he'd expected her response to be to his call—if she had any at all, that is—he certainly hadn't expected her to show up less than twenty-four hours later. She must have booked the nearly six-hour flight from New York to Midland, TX as soon as she'd gotten off the phone with him.

"Can I come in?" She moved forward as she spoke, making it more like a demand than a request, so he took another step back to let her pass.

"Yeah, sure. I'm sorry. I was just surprised to see you."

She turned and glowered at him. "Well, you did call."

There was something accusing in her tone that rankled.

"Yes, but she's been ill for months, Darla. If corporate America couldn't spare you for a day or two in all that time, I didn't expect it to happen now," he snapped.

Darla's hazel eyes seemed to darken. As she glared at him, he took a moment to observe her better. She hadn't changed much since two years ago. She was still slender and smartly dressed. Her blonde, curly hair framed her petite face in the same style as it had before. Her features would almost be soft, but for that intense gaze that always managed to catch him off guard.

Her gaze shifted then and she looked down. That's when he noticed the circles under her eyes.

"I'd like to see my sister now."

****

Darla stepped over the threshold of Lucinda's room and watched her sister water a plant in the window, moving slower than she'd ever seen her move. When she was finished, Lucinda set her pitcher down and paused, as if she sensed Darla's presence. She turned and stared for a whole minute. All at once, Lucinda's features contorted and her eyes turned misty. "Darla!"

Before she knew it, Darla found herself wrapped in her sister's embrace. She closed her arms around Lucinda's frame, her throat closing up. She was so small and frail. "Lucinda, why didn't you tell me?"

Lucinda didn't respond at first. Instead, she pulled away and ambled back to her bed.

Darla sat on the bed beside her, continuing to watch her sister's face.

Finally, Lucinda expelled a heavy breath. "I don't know, Darla. I was so far along when they found out that I didn't even bother with any of the major treatments."

Darla absently smoothed the blanket beside her as she struggled to unravel the explanation. "Were you afraid I'd interfere? Not respect your choice?"

"No, that's not it. See, I knew how it was gonna turn out, and I didn't want to make you watch it . . . not again."

Darla sat up straighter. She didn't have to ask what Lucinda was referring to. "What? This is nothing like what happened to him!"

"You can't even say his name, can you?"

Darla swallowed. "This is nothing like what happened to Jeffrey."

"No, but you'd still have to watch. And I didn't want to put you through that."

Darla's shoulders sagged as her heart clenched. *Always thinking of others.* She slid her hand across the blanket and squeezed Lucinda's. "It's supposed to be the big sister who protects the little one. You didn't need to shield me. I'm made of steel now, ask anyone."

Lucinda gave her a pointed stare. "Then are you ready to talk about Jeffrey?"

Darla flinched in spite of herself. "This isn't the time, is it?"

Lucinda looked away and murmured, "No, not just yet." Her focus returned to Darla. "But don't you ever think of the good times, Darla? What about when we were kids?"

"Of course I do! Sometimes . . ." Honestly, Darla couldn't remember the last time she had thought about their childhood.

They mused in silence together for a while until Lucinda released a soft laugh. "You remember the first time Mama decided we should take a road trip to go see Grandpa in Alabama?"

"How could I forget? All through the South right in the middle of summer. Man!" Darla rubbed her head.

"That's right! Poor Jeffrey's face looked like a little tomato most of the time."

"How old was he then?" Darla asked.

"Still in diapers, 'cuz when we went to . . ."

"That diner!" They said it simultaneously and laughed.

Lucinda wiped her eyes. "The manager got all huffy because Mama didn't order anything before asking where the bathroom was." She waved her arm and deepened her voice to imitate the manager. "'Look, lady, this here's a diner!'"

Darla chuckled. "And what did Mama do? She dangled Jeffrey in the air like a bear cub and yelled, 'This here's a baby with a dirty diaper!'"

Lucinda cracked up. "You sound so much like her!" She paused. "Well, when you're talking normal, anyway. Not when you're using your hoity-toity Manhattan voice."

Darla flapped a dismissive hand at the barb and steered them back to the memory. "Sometimes Mama did things that didn't make much sense. Who ever heard of a woman alone taking three small kids on vacation in a death trap of a car?"

"No, it didn't make much sense but then . . ."

"Then?"

Lucinda's eyes grew misty again. "Don't you remember? Once we made it to the beach near Grandpa's place and saw the water and the sand and the starry night sky, everything made sense. It was like nothing had ever made sense before that."

"Yeah," Darla pondered. "I guess that's why she took us back there every so often. We'd visit right up until Jeffrey . . ." Her jaw snapped shut. No, they weren't going there. No one needed that right now on top of Lucinda's sickness and everything else. "Why don't we pick a different Memory Lane for a bit?"

When there was no response, she looked up to see how her suggestion had gone over. But Lucinda was fast asleep.

6

Clifton's eyes popped open and he stared at the ceiling fan that jingled and creaked as it spun above the rollaway bed he'd set up in the office. He had given up his place in the guest bedroom to Darla, although she had seemed less than overcome with gratitude over his chivalry. She obviously didn't realize that sleeping on a steel beam would have been just as comfortable as the lumps in this foldaway mattress. He croaked out a laugh. *Didn't realize?* No, the more accurate term would probably be "didn't care."

Rolling onto his side, he reached for his phone on the desk beside him. Three fifteen? Hmm. It was surprising he'd lasted that long.

He swung his legs over the bed and climbed to his feet, not sure whether the creaking noises were coming from the bed or his joints. After pulling on his robe, he shuffled out of the office and down the hall to the kitchen. If sleep was out of the question, he'd have to settle for a snack.

He glanced into Lucinda's partially open door as he passed, then did a double take. Her figure, partially outlined by the moonlight trickling through the window, was upright in bed.

Hurrying inside, he flipped on her night table lamp. "Lucinda, what's wrong? Are you in pain?"

Her pale forehead crinkled as she swept widened eyes around the room and finally focused on him. "Clifton?"

He pulled a chair beside her bed and sat down. "I'm here, Lu."

"W-why is it so dark?"

He reached over and squeezed her hand. Her doctor had warned him that Lucinda might be confused sometimes. "It's still night time; almost four a.m."

"Oh . . . okay. Guess I fell asleep while Darla was here." She looked up quickly. "She did come here, right?"

He nodded and rubbed her hand, feeling her tension begin to ease.

Lucinda settled back against her pillows. "It won't be long now."

His hand paused, and he looked up to search her face, but he didn't have to ask what she meant. "I guess not," he murmured, and lowered his head under the weight of her words.

"Hey, listen!" She pulled an exaggerated scowl to mirror his, then reached up and tapped the lines on his forehead until he couldn't help but smile.

"I'm not scared, you know," she assured him.

"Good. I don't think you should be."

They were silent for a while. But then his thoughts began to tumble and turn over the question he'd been wanting to ask. Finally, he leaned closer. "Lu, would you do something for me?"

"Anything. You know that."

He swallowed over the dryness in his throat. "I don't really know how all these things work or what it will be like." His head dropped again. "But, if you see my little girl, will you tell her how much I miss her?"

He glanced up to find that Lucinda's eyes were filled with the tears he'd wished he'd been able to shed for the last three years. She scooted closer and pressed a kiss to his forehead. "Of course I will."

****

Darla steadied her breath and studied what she could see of the large worship space from her place on the front pew. Since she was Lucinda's sister, the funeral director had offered to escort Darla into the room after everyone else was seated and just before the service began. But she had opted to sit down early, so she could have a few moments of silence first, much like she did before Sunday service at her own church. Of course, this community church with its bright lights, sprawling modern space, and worship band instruments was much different from the hundred-year-old sanctuary in New York City. But Darla didn't mind. Lucinda had obviously been an important part of this church community, judging by the number of people waiting in the foyer to come inside and pay their respects.

Closing her eyes, Darla bowed her head and attempted to block out the sound of the canned music playing in the background. Despite the thoughts and feelings swirling inside her, she couldn't seem to focus on a single prayer except a simple, "Thank you."

If nothing else, she was grateful. Lucinda was free from her suffering now and Darla had been given an entire two weeks to spend with her sister before losing her. Enough time for bittersweet reconnecting and reminiscing.

It had been strenuous too. Lucinda's condition had deteriorated quickly soon after Darla's arrival. Neither she nor Clifton had felt comfortable leaving Lucinda alone, so they had taken turns staying up with her.

A rustle of fabric and whispered voices disrupted her thoughts. She raised her head as Clifton came up the aisle followed by two women: a middle-aged redhead and a blonde who was probably the same age but looked younger thanks to her long, perfectly styled hair and glamorous makeup. As soon as the three of them sat down at the other end of Darla's pew, the blonde woman began to rub Clifton's back in an ostensibly comforting gesture.

Darla snorted softly. *Who didn't see that coming?* But almost immediately, she winced at her own cynicism.

Clifton had been a tireless caretaker for her sister, to the point that Lucinda's nurse had remarked that she'd had very little to do because he was so good at handling her prescriptions and meals.

Yet, while Darla was relieved to know that Lucinda was so well cared for, she was also puzzled. Clifton had seemed to accept the difficult work of being in a committed relationship without ever actually committing.

Darla clenched her fist, accidentally crushing the service bulletin in the process. As she straightened it back out, she studied the photo of Lucinda that was printed on the front cover.

If Lucinda had been content with Clifton's status quo, Darla would have let it pass without judgment. But she could tell that wasn't the case from the wistful way Lucinda often spoke about Clifton on the phone. She'd wanted him to marry her.

The ambient worship music abruptly spiked by several decibels, then cut off entirely. A young pastor in a suit and loosely knotted necktie stepped up to the pulpit and beamed. "Good morning, family. I want to thank you all for coming out today to celebrate the life of our sister, Lucinda. Such a sweet, sweet lady and a huge part of our church! We're really going to miss her, but we know she's in a beautiful place now, and so I hope you'll rejoice with me in that assurance."

The pastor's remarks set the tone for the rest of the service, which consisted of upbeat music interspersed with memories shared by friends and former coworkers from Lucinda's days as an elementary school secretary. It was a sharp contrast from the solemn and reverent liturgies Darla had attended after the death of friends at her own church, but it seemed to fit Lucinda's personality. Once everyone was finished speaking, a large screen behind the pulpit blinked to life and displayed the same photo that adorned the bulletin.

Darla tensed. This was the part where they'd play the slideshow the funeral home had compiled from Lucinda's photos. She set the bulletin aside and laced her fingers together in her lap, bracing for the onslaught of memories.

But a moment later, she nearly jumped out of her seat as a lively recording of horns and guitars filled the room. The slideshow had been set to the song "Alive Again" by Chicago, one of Lucinda's favorite bands when she was younger. Darla stared at the screen and forced her mouth to stop hanging open.

Catching movement in her peripheral vision, she turned her head and spotted Clifton watching her. Their eyes met, and he surprised her by sending a small, apologetic smile.

She responded with a shrug. It was what Lucinda had wanted. Unconventional or not, the exuberant love song of renewal seemed oddly fitting, and Darla found herself smiling through the succession of old photos she'd been dreading only a moment before.

7

After shaking dozens of hands and returning numerous hugs from Lucinda's friends, Clifton was relieved to finally be leaving the church. When he spotted Darla in the front hall of the worship building, he approached and offered to walk her out. She accepted, perhaps realizing, like he did, that they still had a few matters to settle regarding Lucinda's house and belongings.

As the two of them headed toward the exit in silence, Luther Palmer, Lucinda's attorney, appeared directly in front of them and blocked their progress.

The tall seventy-something-year-old black man with his impeccably pressed three-piece suit and gold horn-rimmed glasses was the picture of an old-school attorney.

He raised his hands in a placating gesture. "I'm sorry, Ms. Mayhew," he nodded to Darla and turned to Clifton, "and Mr. Peters, but I'm afraid there's one more matter of business that needs to be discussed."

Darla huffed a tired sigh. "Mr. Palmer, I thought we settled all of this already."

Clifton thought so too. What little savings Lucinda had left had been directed to various charities, per her last wishes, as would the proceeds from the sale of her house when it happened. He had moved back to his own apartment and Darla was already making progress sorting through the things Lucinda had left behind.

Mr. Palmer removed his glasses. "Maybe 'business' is the wrong word. You see, what we need to discuss is the matter of Ms.

Lucinda's remains."

Darla frowned. "I assumed her ashes would stay in my possession."

"Actually, she had very specific instructions about that, but asked that I wait until all the other arrangements were made because she didn't want to overtax you."

He pulled an envelope from his inside coat pocket. "Pastor Murray offered the use of one of the Sunday school rooms, so if you don't mind, I'd like to explain the request now."

The classroom was small, but well lit and comfortably furnished with a sofa and cushiony chairs rather than tables or desks. Once they were seated, Mr. Palmer pulled a paper from the envelope and scanned it. "She asked that her ashes be scattered off the Gulf Coast at sunrise, near the town where her grandfather once lived."

Mr. Palmer eyed Darla over his glasses. "She said you would remember the place, Ms. Mayhew."

Darla's expression turned grave, but she nodded. "Yes, it was near Point Clear, Alabama. She was fond of that place when we were young." Scooting toward the edge of her chair, she said, "I will take the first available flight down there."

"Uh, wait just a moment, Ms. Mayhew," Mr. Palmer raised his hand. "It's not that simple. She wants you both to drive down there . . . on a road trip like the ones you took with your mother."

Clifton sank back deeper into his chair. Lucinda had entrusted him with this too? She really—

"I'm sorry, Mr. Palmer," Darla's cold and incredulous tone cut into his reflections. "Did you say both of us?" She stared at the man as if he'd said Lucinda had wanted them to circumnavigate the globe in a rowboat.

"Yes, ma'am. That's what she said."

Clifton scowled at Darla's overblown response, but he addressed the attorney respectfully. "Thank you, Mr. Palmer. For my part, I would be honored to carry out Lucinda's final wish."

"Will you excuse us a moment?" Darla blurted out before facing him, her intense brown eyes practically flashing with irritation. "Clifton, could we talk in the hall?"

She stood and swept out of the room without even stopping to see if he was following her.

Clifton mumbled an apology to Mr. Palmer and trailed after

Darla.

Once they were in the hall, she whirled around. "I appreciate your willingness to help, Clifton, but you don't need to trouble yourself."

"Trouble myself?" He planted his hands on his waist. "Didn't you hear what Mr. Palmer said? It's what she wanted! Do you expect me to just shrug off the responsibility?"

Darla's brow dipped in a frown. "What responsibility? You aren't family. There are no legalities involved. You're under no obligation."

Clifton's pulse began to pound in his ears, and he leaned in close until they were eye to eye. "How dare you talk to me like that? I cared about Lucinda! We were companions. And more importantly, I was by her side from the day the doctor told her she only had months to live until the end. I even walked away from my work to look after her!"

He inched forward. "But that's not something you'd understand, is it? Putting relationships before your career?"

She stared at him for a moment, then lowered her eyes, wincing almost imperceptibly. "Relationships . . ." she murmured, more to herself than to him. When she looked up again, her face had grown drawn and tired. "If you insist on going through with this, we should probably plan to leave as soon as possible. I have to get back to my work, after all."

His stomach sank a little as he regarded her. What was wrong with him? Whatever he thought of Darla, it was completely inappropriate for him to be berating her at her sister's funeral like this. He softened his voice. "Darla, I—"

But without giving him another glance, she turned on her heel and stalked back to the classroom.

****

Darla pulled her rented sedan into Lucinda's driveway and turned off the engine, but she didn't get out or even loosen the vise grip she'd had on the steering wheel ever since she'd sped out of the church parking lot. Why would Lucinda leave such absurd final demands?

It would have been no trouble to take a flight down to the Gulf and release her sister's ashes like she'd wanted. Why a road trip? What possible difference could it make to Lucinda how her remains got to their final resting place? And why, why, why would Lucinda ever think it was a good idea for her and Clifton to go together? Was this some kind of a practical joke? A life lesson?

Darla groaned. None of it made the least bit of sense. As she continued sitting, her focus settled on the neatly landscaped bushes and flowerbeds in the front yard. The blossoms were lovely, and it wasn't hard to see Lucinda's personal touch in selecting them. She'd always had a knack for planting and nurturing things, whether it was plants or people.

Why did it feel like Lucinda's last wishes were to make her own sister part of some human landscaping project?

Darla expelled a heavy breath and reached for her purse. As she did, it started to vibrate, so she unzipped it and pulled her phone from its designated pocket. When Natalie's name flashed across the screen, Darla hesitated. Normally, she wouldn't talk to anyone when she was this agitated, but she had a sudden urge to hear a friendly voice.

"Hey, Natalie."

"Darla, hi. Is this a bad time?"

"No." Darla grabbed her purse and got out of the car. "I just got back from the memorial service."

There was a long beat of silence, then, "So your sister passed away? I'm so sorry. And I'm sorry for not calling earlier. I just didn't want to bother you."

The kindness in Natalie's voice spread through Darla's heart like the sunbeams scattering through the leaves of the tree she walked under as she made her way to the front door. "There's no need to apologize, Natalie. It happened quickly but peacefully."

"How are you feeling now?"

Darla released a dry chuckle as she opened the front door and stepped in the house. "Too many things to name, I think."

"No doubt," Natalie murmured. "How did the memorial go?"

"The service itself went fine. After that . . ." Impulsively, Darla plopped down on the sofa and spilled the whole story about Mr. Palmer, Lucinda's request, and even her argument with Clifton.

When she was finished, Natalie said, "Wow! Her request sounds really involved."

"Yeah, I just don't know why it has to involve Clifton," Darla grumbled, trying to ignore the fact that she sounded like a petulant child.

"You really dislike him, don't you?"

"No! Why would you say that?" Darla deadpanned.

Natalie's laugh tinkled through the speaker. "It's just an impression I got. But it won't be that bad, will it? It's only for a couple of days. You can't possibly argue the whole time!"

"Humph. You'd be surprised. But his arguing might be better than his civility. I have a feeling he'll either drone on some more about his devotion to Lucinda or he'll make small talk like he did when they visited me two years ago."

"Small talk?"

"Yes, I took them to the Metropolitan Museum of Art, and he took over the tour with endless facts. He seemed to know something about every single exhibit, and then he kept talking about the places he'd traveled for work and asking if I'd been to them. When I said I hadn't, he acted all snooty and appalled that I stayed in one place building my career like a grownup instead of gallivanting around the globe!"

Darla paused to catch her breath after her invective. It was hard to say, but it almost sounded like Natalie was stifling a snicker.

Her face warmed. "I'm sorry, Natalie. I didn't mean to carry on like that."

"No! It's okay. It's best to let it out now. Then you'll be fine on the trip."

"What makes you so sure?"

"I know you, Darla. You've spent your whole career fighting for success and earning the respect of obtuse men. Yet you've still managed to come through all of that with an amazingly big heart."

Darla paused and frowned at the phone, an immediate denial rising to her lips, but she didn't voice it. Instead, she let Natalie's words sink all the way in. "Do you really think that?"

"Absolutely!"

"Oh. Well . . . thank you."

"You're welcome. Now, I should go and let you get some rest, but please keep me updated, okay?"

"Okay." Darla ended the call and leaned her head against the back of the sofa. Natalie was right. Darla was no stranger to dealing with difficult men, and she could certainly deal with Clifton for a few days. Once it was over, she'd never have to see him again.

8

Clifton bent down to check the air pressure and tread of his tires for the final time, not expecting to find any issues. The day before, he'd had his favorite mechanic do a comprehensive inspection of the tires, belts, and fluids. He was determined to ensure nothing went wrong with the trip and that Darla would have no legitimate reason to complain.

After a few minutes, he stood up with a grunt and ran his hand over the electric blue body of his refurbished 1965 Shelby Mustang. Noticing a spot on the window, he grabbed a cloth. As he wiped, he caught sight of his reflection in the glass and shook his head at himself. When had he ever allowed anyone or anything to get under his skin like Darla did? It just wasn't his way. In over twenty years of handling architecture projects in all kinds of places, working with all kinds of people, he'd always managed to remain easygoing and even-tempered. But for some reason, it was different with Darla.

Maybe it was her open disapproval of him and his relationship with Lucinda. Maybe it was the fact that Darla had the audacity to disapprove of anything, when she'd barely involved herself with Lucinda's life. Whatever it was, he resolved not to let it vex him anymore.

If Darla wanted to cause problems, she'd be on her own. For his part, he would be considerate and well-behaved.

He did a final once-over of his Mustang, his chest filling with pride the way it always did when he took a moment to admire the car, then he slid into the driver's seat and headed to Lucinda's house to meet Darla.

When he arrived at the agreed upon time, Darla was already rolling her suitcase onto the driveway.

Clifton parked and jumped out to help. "Morning."

"Yes, it is."

He ignored her dry non-greeting. "Can I put your case in the trunk for you?"

"Thanks."

She regarded the car then, and raised an eyebrow. "A midlife crisis mobile. Why am I not surprised?"

His hand clenched around the handle of the suitcase he'd just picked up and he closed his eyes. *Just a joke, Peters. Just a joke.*

Without pausing, he continued toward the car and opened the trunk. "Nah. That title would have to go to my Harley." He placed the suitcase in the trunk and peeked around the lid. "We could take that, if you'd prefer?"

While Darla didn't laugh, she condescended to smirk. "No. I'd like to keep all my limbs, if you don't mind."

"Right."

The mild amusement on Darla's face faded as she turned and walked back into the house. When she came back, she was carrying the bamboo box that held Lucinda's remains.

Clifton stepped back so she could place them into the car as she chose, and a deep, inner fatigue pulled on him as he watched. Even after she'd finished, he couldn't seem to move, as if his feet were buried in quick-drying concrete. Darla remained still too.

Finally, he managed to shake off his immobility. He cleared his throat. "Shall we?"

She nodded and made her way to the passenger side of the car, but then she hesitated. "Clifton, there's something I should tell you before we go." She looked away and puffed out a breath. "I can't ride in the car for more than two hours at a time. That is to say, I have to take a half-hour break or so in between. And even then, I can't go more than four or five hours in one day."

Startled, he said, "Oh. Do you get carsick or something?"

"No. I have a problem with my lower back. The pain gets sharp if I sit for too long. I had an appointment to get surgery on it, but it didn't fit into my schedule, so I had to put it off."

Clearly, Darla neglected more than her sister in the interest of her work schedule.

He started to do calculations in his head. With that many stops throughout the day, there was a good chance this trip would take two or three days longer than he had anticipated. Why hadn't Darla told him this before? Was she hoping he'd decide to back out of the trip because of the last-minute schedule change? Well, it wasn't going to work.

He shrugged. "All right, I understand. We will make plans to stop every two hours. But be sure to let me know if you need to take a break a little bit sooner if you get too uncomfortable at any point."

Her eyes widened a little, but she nodded. "I will. Thanks." She shifted her feet and bent to pick up a long pillow that he had not noticed before. Her face reddened slightly as she placed it in the passenger seat. Her obvious discomfiture suggested that she was embarrassed by her infirmity or embarrassed to own up to it, at least. Maybe that's why she didn't talk about it sooner. Lucinda had told him on more than one occasion that Darla was a proud woman. In deference to that pride, he stopped staring and focused on getting himself in the car.

Any expectation Clifton had that the slight courtesy Darla had shown while they were preparing to leave would expand into friendlier discourse as the journey continued was soon put to rest.

She spent most of the first half hour alternating between reading and scribbling something in a notebook—probably work she'd brought from her office. None of his attempts at polite conversation had elicited any more than a two- or three-word response from her. Since Lucinda was the only thing they seemed to have in common, he started with a few entertaining memories of their time together. *He* thought they were entertaining, anyway.

But Darla did not appear to be entertained. So then he moved on to small talk. He shared some of the interesting but little-known tidbits he had picked up from his travels, particularly the ones that related to the trajectory they were taking for this trip. Rather than two- or three-word responses, her replies to these were more monosyllabic in nature.

He finally gave up and switched on his stereo. When he'd had the Mustang refurbished, he had paid extra for a completely modern Bluetooth sound system. When he flipped the switch, the Beatles' "Ticket to Ride" burst through the speakers, making Darla jump. He hastily turned the volume down. "Sorry about that."

The music continued to play at a reasonable volume. After a second, Darla looked up from her reading and gazed at the stereo display.

He rubbed his left temple, which was threatening to ache. "Is the music disturbing you? I can turn it off," he reluctantly offered, as he reached for the dial.

"No, don't." She held up her hand. "I mean, it's your car."

She didn't go back to reading as he'd anticipated. Instead, she continued looking straight ahead with her eyes half closed.

"Wait a minute," he exclaimed. "Don't tell me we actually have something in common!"

Darla's eyes opened, and she frowned. "Pardon?"

He grinned with an enthusiasm he didn't quite understand. "I said it looks like we enjoy the same kind of music. You're a Beatles fan too."

She went back to reading. "I imagine lots of people are."

He sighed and returned his focus to the road. *Well, that was six words, at least.*

9

Darla paced the grassy perimeter of the rest area, relieved when her limping gradually turned into something more like her usual gait, and the tension that cramped her back loosened up.

With another ten minutes of walking and maybe a stretch or two, she'd be ready for a couple more hours in the car. As she made her way to a less conspicuous spot to stretch, she wiped the perspiration from her forehead. How could she have forgotten how muggy Texas is, even in the spring?

She passed clusters of vacationing families and leashed dogs with their tongues hanging out until she found an out-of-the-way picnic table. Just as she put her purse down on the table's bench, the sound of a throaty male voice carried from somewhere on the other side of the restroom facility building.

"Hey, beautiful, what's your name?"

"None of your business," another voice snapped. This one sounded like it belonged to a girl or young woman.

"All right, how 'bout I just keep calling you 'beautiful,' then?"

"Whatever. I have to go."

There was a slight scuffling sound, followed by, "Wait, what's your hurry, beautiful? I'll bet you need a ride, don't you? You and I could—"

"Let go of me!"

Darla jolted to attention and hurried toward the sound of the voices. She rounded the corner of the building where a large, grizzly man towered over a willowy brown-haired girl who couldn't have been any older than seventeen or eighteen.

"Excuse me!" Darla butted in. "What is going on here?"

The man jumped back like he'd been burned, and the girl took that as her chance to put even more distance between them. But she didn't run away.

The man turned on Darla and glowered. "And who are you, her mom?"

Darla marched forward. "What if I am?"

He sent a dubious glance toward the girl, who was bending over to pick up the backpack she must have dropped in the scuffle. She also had a guitar case at her feet with the name "Jess" painted in white letters on the side facing Darla.

"Come on, Jessica, grab your stuff and let's go. We're already running late."

The girl straightened and looked at Darla with wide, startling green eyes. "Um, yeah, okay. Sorry to be so slow."

"Wait a minute," the big man piped up. "I don't think—"

Clifton materialized then, holding two cans of soda. "Ready, ladies?" he chirped.

He stepped forward and handed them each a can. "I'm afraid all the machine had left was diet orange soda."

The man's mouth fell open, making his scraggly beard dip down to the neck of his faded black t-shirt. Clifton ignored him and urged Darla and the girl to walk in front of him with a wide sweep of his arm.

The girl hurried ahead but Darla hung back and strolled beside him. When they were out of the big man's earshot, she leaned toward Clifton and murmured, "Nice move. But how'd you know to show up like that?"

"I heard a commotion." He shrugged. "Somehow I knew you'd be involved."

Darla glared at him, which prompted a grin, as if he'd been anticipating her reaction.

When they got to the car, Clifton perched on the hood, crossed his arms, and looked at the girl. "So, is your name actually Jessica?"

"Yes, sir. Thank you both for your help." She tucked her hair behind her ear and grimaced. "That guy was a creep."

Darla asked, "Are you here alone?"

She raised her chin. "Yes, ma'am. I'm hitchhiking to Pensacola, Florida to see my mom. My last ride was only going to Abilene, so

I asked them to drop me off here."

Darla's eyes met Clifton's, and his face wrinkled with the same concern that was winding through her stomach.

Jessica seemed to be reading their reaction because she held up her hands and laughed. "Hey, come on, it's not that bad! Hitchhiking is not as dangerous as they make it look on TV. It's more dangerous just driving a car, but that doesn't stop anyone, does it?"

Darla knew better than to argue with naivete. She shifted to lean against the car beside where Clifton sat. "I hadn't thought of it that way. In any case, why don't you get a ride with us? We're going to Point Clear, Alabama. Do you know where that is?"

Jessica's face brightened. "It's only fifty or sixty miles from where I'm going!"

Darla turned to Clifton. His eyes were bulging as he tripped to his feet. "Will you excuse us for a second, Jessica?"

He placed his hand on Darla's arm and tugged her with him across the parking lot. When they were a few yards away, he came to an abrupt stop and stared hard at her. It was the same way he'd confronted her when they'd quarreled after the memorial. Why did he have to stand so close, staring straight into her eyes? It was unsettling yet almost magnetic at the same time.

"Have you lost your senses?" he demanded.

Darla's arm began to tingle, and she looked down to see his hand still holding her. "Do you mind?" she said, pulling away.

"I'm sorry." He quickly released her. "But my question stands. Have. You. Lost. Your. Senses? That girl is obviously a runaway or something, and you want to harbor her?"

He waved his hand in the air. "We could get in trouble with the law. Do you realize that? I'm sure as a corporate lawyer, you know more about bending the law than following it, but I'm not comfortable with this!"

Her fists balled. "I hate to disappoint you, Clifton, but I'm a law-abiding citizen and I understand what harboring is! But I don't think you're completely appreciating how dangerous hitchhiking can be for a girl her age."

"I'm aware of the dangers. I have a teenage daughter." He went still, and his forehead crumpled. "Had. I had a teenage daughter." His voice trailed off.

All at once, Darla's memory slid back to the day Lucinda had told her about first meeting Clifton. She'd said he had been divorced for several years and that his only child, a fourteen-year-old girl, had died a few months before Lucinda had met him.

Darla swallowed. How could she have forgotten a detail like that?

Clifton seemed to have composed himself while Darla mused, and he went right on talking as if there'd been no interruption. "I would have never wanted my daughter in a situation like this. That's why I think we should find out if this girl really is a runaway. Then, we can persuade her to go to the authorities and—"

"No!" Darla's hands went clammy at the thought.

Her outburst seemed to have shocked Clifton into silence, so she followed up on the advantage. "No authorities. Look, I have a friend who can help. We can get a few more details from the girl and he'll be able to look her up in all the databases for missing and runaway kids. Meanwhile, if we give her a lift, she'll be safe."

Clifton was still standing close, but he didn't look angry or appalled any more. His expression was grave and he searched her eyes, as if seeking the answer to a puzzle. For reasons she couldn't quite understand, his scrutiny made her pulse pick up.

Finally, he sighed and moved away. "Fine. I'm not sure I like it, but I'll go along for now."

10

When they turned to rejoin Jessica, it was clear from her tense posture that she'd been watching their conversation carefully, but Clifton was fairly certain she hadn't overheard it.

He sent the girl what he hoped was a reassuring smile. "Well, Ms. Jessica, let's make some room for your stuff, shall we?"

Relief swept over her face, and she beamed. "Oh, thanks! Thank you, both."

"It's no trouble, dear," Darla assured her. "My name's Darla by the way, and this is Clifton."

Finding a place for Jessica's luggage wasn't any trouble, at least. She only had a backpack and guitar case, and she wanted to keep those in the backseat beside her. Within a couple of minutes, they were all settled in the car.

"Are you ready to go?" Clifton asked Darla.

"Why wouldn't I be ready to go?"

Clifton tightened his lips. "Alrighty then."

As they started driving, Jessica leaned toward the front seat. "How long have you two been married, anyway?"

"We're not!" Clifton and Darla said simultaneously.

"That's a relief." The remark was followed by a popping noise, and Clifton glanced in the rearview mirror to see that Jessica had clapped her hand over her mouth. "Sorry," she mumbled.

Clifton cast a side-glance at Darla, and she responded with one of the few genuine smiles he'd ever seen from her. "That's all right, Jessica. No one is more relieved than we are."

He slapped his hand on the wheel and laughed, with Jessica joining in a second later.

When things were quiet again, Darla shifted and glanced over her shoulder. "So, you play the guitar?"

"Yes, ma'am."

Darla chuckled. "I appreciate your manners, Jessica, but you don't have to call me 'ma'am.' 'Darla' is fine."

Clifton pulled an overly earnest face and looked at the rearview mirror. "I'd rather you didn't call me 'ma'am' either."

Jessica giggled and Darla ignored him. She asked, "How long have you played?"

"Since I was six or seven, so almost ten years now, I guess."

Clifton grasped the steering wheel harder. She *was* a minor.

"Hmm. That's impressive," Darla mused. "What kind of music do you play?"

"It's pretty eclectic. I like to play blues, folk, acoustic rock . . . whatever tunes speak to me."

"How about oldies?" Clifton chimed in. "Do you like the Beatles?"

"Sure. Lots of people do."

He glanced at Darla long enough to see her smirk.

"That's right, Clifton. Lots of people do." Returning her attention to Jessica, Darla asked, "Do you ever perform for an audience?"

"I have a few times. And I have a YouTube channel."

"Ah! So you have an online audience," Darla replied, pulling out her phone. "I'd like to check out your channel; may I ask what it's called?"

"Sure!" Jessica's young voice went up an excited octave. "It's called 'Jess's Heart Songs.'"

"Catchy name," Clifton remarked.

Darla tapped on her phone. "Found it. I'll bookmark this and watch it when I'm on Wi-Fi later. It looks like you have a good number of subscribers. That's great."

"Thanks."

Jessica continued talking about her music, but Clifton was distracted by the tapping noises coming from Darla's phone. He peeked over in time to see her start a text with Jessica's name in the message, along with a screenshot of a video.

Then she gave him a thumbs up. He forced a smile in response.

There was something alarmingly efficient about this woman. Right now, she was using that attribute for good. But why did it feel like she could just as easily use it to break a heart, if she had a mind to?

Practically unbidden, a memory returned of Lucinda mentioning that Darla had been engaged once years ago, but that it hadn't ended well. Had Darla dispensed with some guy as quickly and easily as she'd gleaned personal information from this young girl for her friend to investigate? Were people expendable to her? She certainly hadn't prioritized her sick sister until the last possible moment.

After a second, Clifton gave his head a shake. What right did he have to speculate on Darla's past or judge her relationship decisions? His personal life was certainly no beacon of success.

Darla continued conversing with Jessica until the girl's voice grew soft and a little groggy. "It's okay, Jessica," Darla said. "You can take a nap if you want. There's no need to stay awake just to keep the old fogies entertained."

"You guys aren't old. You know what YouTube is," Jessica countered.

Clifton nodded. "She has a point."

Once Jessica had gone to sleep, Clifton did a quick scan of the passenger seat beside him. Darla wasn't moving around, messing with her cushion, or doing anything else to indicate she was getting uncomfortable, but he checked anyway. "Is everything all right? Do you need to take a break?"

"I'm fine. That walk around the rest area really helped. I should be okay until Fort Worth."

"Sounds good."

She pulled her book from her bag, but before she could start reading again, he interrupted her. "You're pretty good with kids."

"Oh, I guess that's just a habit by now. I work with teens at my church. Didn't Lucinda ever mention that?"

"She did," he acknowledged. "But I guess I always pictured it being like a *Scared Straight* kind of thing, where you march around in army fatigues and yell."

"Keep your fantasies to yourself, please."

He barked out a shocked laugh, then covered his mouth, and checked to be sure he hadn't disturbed Jessica. She was quiet and still.

As he faced forward again, he said, "Tell me about the kids."

Darla didn't reply for an entire minute. He wasn't sure if she was reluctant to tell him anything or surprised that he would take an interest. "Aw, come on," he wheedled. "We have to keep this old fogey awake, after all."

For once, he must've succeeded at being disarming because she began to tell him.

As she talked, he nearly forgot to pay attention to the road several times because he was so taken aback.

It wasn't what she talked about that was so surprising; it was *the way* she talked about it. Her tone brightened, and her face relaxed. She beamed with pride as she described the things the kids learned and accomplished. And she even threw her head back and laughed as she described her bumbling first attempts at befriending them when she'd started working on the program.

It was like he was finally getting a glimpse of the Darla that Lucinda had loved and admired so much. And truthfully, he was floored.

Determined to keep her chatting on this topic she was so passionate about, he asked, "Do you do Bible studies or Sunday school lessons with the kids too?"

"We do some of that, yes. There are all kinds of curriculums available, but I didn't realize that when we started, so I just adapted the adult lessons into something I thought the kids would find more relatable to their own experiences. It seemed to work well, so I kept doing it. In fact, that's what I'm working on here." She gestured at the book and notebook in her lap. "This will be for Vacation Bible School at the end of the summer."

"Oh, I see."

So she wasn't just dragging her business around with her. And, despite what he'd always presumed, there was more to her life in Manhattan than a career.

The car fell silent. Darla seemed to be deep in thought, reflecting on her time with the youth, perhaps.

Clifton pensively swept his eyes from side to side, taking in the sprawling fields dotted with wildflowers and carpeted with grass that was lush and green, thanks to recent rains. Some of the rows of crops were still partially immersed in water that was as muddied as his thoughts were at the moment.

The more he considered everything Darla had discussed with

him, the more his image of her shifted. Yet one question returned to plague him over and over. He needed to let it go. He should have let it go already, but it was impossible.

"Darla?"

"Hmm?"

"I know it's none of my business. You'll probably tell me it's none of my business . . . again, that is. But I just can't understand why you didn't come see Lucinda sooner when she was so sick. Now that I've been around you more, I can't see you staying away when you knew that."

Darla didn't look at him. Her voice was low and quiet when she said, "I didn't know."

He snapped his head toward her and stared. "What was that?"

"I didn't know she was sick."

His gut clenched. "Th-that can't be. You two talked every week. She must have told you when she was diagnosed, or about her consultations with the doctors?"

Darla remained silent.

"Nothing?" He drew in a shaky breath. "So, the first you knew that your sister was dying was when I screamed at you over the phone about it?"

She gazed out the window without making a response.

"Darla, I am so sorry. I—"

"Forget it," she cut him off.

"I can't forget it! I was a complete jerk to you."

"Clifton, just drop it, okay? I needed to know. How I found out is irrelevant."

"Okay, I won't bring it up anymore."

She went back to her book and didn't acknowledge him again for the rest of the drive to Fort Worth. He was left with a nagging sense that whatever progress they'd made toward a friendlier dynamic had been crushed like the soda can he'd run over a few minutes before.

****

Clifton held back the curtain of his hotel window and gazed out, but it afforded him very little distraction from his churning thoughts.

When they'd arrived at the small, moderately priced hotel he and Darla had selected prior to starting the trip, they had both offered to pay for an extra room for Jessica. But she had objected, suggesting she sleep in the car instead. After a few more minutes of deliberating, Darla came up with the clever solution to upgrade her own room to a suite with an adjoining living area and sofa bed and allowing Jessica to pay the small difference for the upgrade.

When the matter of the hotel had been resolved, Clifton suggested they all go to dinner, but Darla preferred to get something to-go for them to take back to their hotel rooms. He couldn't be sure if she was avoiding further interaction with him or if she was simply tired from the first day's journey. Whichever the case was, he was now alone in his room with nothing but a half-eaten burger and regret to keep him company.

And, after today, he had enough regret to construct an impressive tower of it. Despite barely knowing her, he had been so biased against Darla that he'd never even considered there might be an explanation for her not visiting Lucinda—other than that she couldn't be bothered with it. Now, he could see how absurd that had been. The way he'd talked to her on the phone had been little short of cruel.

A faint rumbling drew his attention to the sky outside, where a mass of gray rolled over the top of the distant buildings. They were probably in for overnight storms. Foreboding reached all the way to Clifton's heart.

He had another, deeper regret. There was a good chance he had ruined the tenuous connection he'd been forming with Darla. That disturbed him more than he understood.

Maybe it was because he knew how much it would've disappointed Lucinda. Or maybe it was because he was just beginning to respect Darla. When she'd talked so freely earlier, he'd even gotten a crazy notion that they could end up friends.

But he'd managed to sabotage that possibility.

An outside movement drew his focus to the window once more. He was startled to see Jessica walking across the hotel courtyard and past the pool, until she reached a set of lawn chairs partially obscured by hedges. She sat down and pulled out her guitar.

After a few moments of tuning, she began to pluck the strings. Even behind the window glass, he could hear the notes as she began to play and sing a slow, plaintive rendition of "Eleanor

Rigby." The chords and lyrics of the Beatles' classic ballad of loneliness wafted through the evening air like ghosts. He swallowed a painful lump in his throat and gripped the curtain he'd been holding back.

He was about to back away when he noticed an open window across the courtyard. Leaning closer to the pane, he spotted Darla looking out toward Jessica like he had been a moment earlier. As if sensing his scrutiny, she turned and looked straight at him.

He paused, wondering if he should wave or nod, but she didn't give him the chance. She moved away from the window and snapped the curtains shut.

Jessica's sonorous voice continued to echo through the courtyard. *All the lonely people.*

11

Darla drizzled cream over the morning's second cup of coffee and swirled it around with a spoon. She took a sip and closed her eyes. *Mmm.* It was just diner java, and not the $6.88 coffee shop brew she often got in Manhattan, but it was almost as good.

She opened her eyes and froze. Clifton was watching her from across the table, an inscrutable expression on his face. When she returned his regard, he looked away.

Strange.

Clearing her throat, she said, "I guess we'd better get going. We have a long day ahead."

She turned to Jessica, who was scooping up her last bite of oatmeal. "I'm sorry we have to take this trip so slowly, Jessica. You probably didn't realize you were signing up for an extended journey."

Jessica gave a tiny shrug and finished the oatmeal. "It beats flying."

"What? Really?" Clifton asked.

"Sure. Who wants to fly? Cramped seats, layovers, doll-sized bags of pretzels. This is much better."

Darla laughed, then took another sip of her coffee just as their short and stocky, gray-headed server approached.

"One check, please, and I'll take it," Clifton said.

"Got it." The man started off.

Darla set her coffee down with a thud. "Now wait a minute, I'd like my own check, sir."

The server halted and returned to the table.

Clifton lowered his voice. "Come on, Darla, let me pay for the food. It's the least I can do when—"

Her pulse picked up in an irritated rhythm. "You don't need to *do* anything. I'm perfectly capable of paying for my own."

"No one said you weren't! But don't be silly. There's no need for separate checks." He looked at the server, whose head was bobbing back and forth between them. "Just one check."

Clifton's dismissive attitude piqued her. "I am *not* being silly. I—"

"Guys, chill!" Jessica spoke up in a tone much louder than her usual one. "Why don't you take turns paying the check like you do for gas?"

Darla couldn't help but gape at the girl and her no-nonsense exclamation. Clifton blinked and rubbed the back of his neck. "Gee. I guess that would be the simplest thing, wouldn't it?"

He looked at Darla. She nodded.

"Good." He grinned at her. "And just to show you my chivalry, I'll let you pay first."

Returning his attention to the server, he said, "Please put the three meals on one check, sir, and bring it to the lady."

"Hey! I can pay for my own oatmeal," Jessica broke in with an offended tone.

"Aw, for cryin' out loud!" The waiter slapped his palm on his forehead and stomped away.

The three of them stared after him.

Jessica snickered first, then Clifton chortled. Pretty soon they were all giggling.

"Goodness, you'd normally have to go on a lion safari to see this kind of pride," Darla quipped.

Clifton snorted and looked at Jessica. "Oh, man." He gestured at Darla. "And she acts like *my* jokes are corny."

Once they had settled down, Darla said, "Look, why don't we do meals for now, and you get the tip, Jessica? And better make it a good one; we've caused that guy a lot of trouble."

While Darla and Jessica finally settled the tab, Clifton excused himself to go check on the car.

Since their table was next to the window, Darla could see Clifton in the parking lot. He kicked the tires for a minute, then grabbed a cloth from the trunk to polish the hood.

Darla shook her head. That man was batty about his car.

Of course, he couldn't possibly act as batty as she had. What on earth was wrong with her—causing a scene over something as trifling as a restaurant bill?

The problem wasn't the bill, though. It was the fact that she'd sensed he was trying to apologize again like he had the night before. And she still didn't know what to do with it.

Right from the start, she'd known that Clifton hadn't meant to be the first one to tell her of Lucinda's condition, but frankly, she doubted it would have mattered to him if he *had* known.

But his broaching the subject of that phone call had caught her off guard. Things had almost turned friendly between them when they'd talked about her work with the kids. It had softened her. Maybe too much. Clifton's remorse had overwhelmed her. She didn't doubt its sincerity. In fact, she'd had the strangest urge to talk about that day; to let go and walk through the shock and sorrow of finding out Lucinda was ill with the one person who would understand.

But she couldn't.

"What's the deal with you two, anyway?"

Darla started and faced Jessica. She'd almost forgotten the girl was there. "What do you mean?"

Jessica twisted the end of her hair around her finger. "I mean, you guys aren't married or a couple, so what are you?"

Darla frowned. She'd been so busy fishing for information from Jessica, trying to find out if she was a runaway, that she hadn't bothered to offer any explanation of her own. That didn't seem right.

So as simply as she could, Darla told Jessica why she and Clifton were headed to the Gulf Coast.

When she finished, Jessica's brow was knit in deep concentration. "That's what's in the bamboo box, huh?"

"Yeah. I'm sorry. It must all sound rather strange to someone your age. Does it bother you?"

Jessica shook her head. "You two must have really loved your sister to do this for her."

Darla released a shaky breath. "Well, it's the last thing we *can* do for her."

Tears glistened in Jessica's surprising green eyes. "It's beautiful."

As they stood to leave, Darla hung back and observed the girl. She was a sensitive, intelligent young woman. If she was a runaway, someone must surely be missing her.

****

Jessica and Darla wandered out to the parking lot and watched Clifton kick his tires for a few minutes longer. Darla smirked. If nothing else, their absurd little tiff in the diner had probably convinced Clifton not to make any more apology attempts. That was a relief.

Once Clifton realized they were both watching him, he stood up straight and sheepishly asked, "Why didn't y'all tell me you were ready to go?"

He focused on Darla then, and his expression sobered. Reaching into his pocket, he pulled out the car keys and slowly extended them to her. "Darla, would you like to drive for a while?"

Darla felt her jaw go slack. "You want *me* to drive your car?"

He nodded once.

Darla crossed her arms. "You do realize I spent most of the last thirty years taking cabs and subways, right?"

His Adam's apple bobbed as he swallowed. "Y-yeah, but you were getting around Midland all right in your rental, weren't you? So I guess it's like riding a bike."

"You're sure?"

"Yeah. I trust you."

Everything inside her went still at his words, but she managed to reach out and accept the keys from him. Who knew that an olive branch would come with a Shelby Mustang keychain attached to it?

It didn't take long to get used to the car. Darla was no automotive expert, but it seemed that the Mustang had been skillfully refurbished since it basically drove like a contemporary car. What she hadn't been expecting was the burst of power that emanated from the engine as she accelerated onto the interstate. Her heart rate fluttered and picked up, and a smile tickled the corners of her mouth.

The sound of Clifton's chuckle caught her attention, and she glanced over to see him grinning at her reaction. "You gotta admit it's fun, right?"

"Yeah, it's pretty fun."

His laugh deepened at the admission. It was a nice sound. That was another thing she could admit, although that didn't mean she'd announce it.

They drove in silence for a few minutes until Clifton said, "I heard you playing and singing last night, Jessica. You're good."

"Thanks!" she replied.

"I know you said you'd been playing for a while, but it sounds like you have natural talent too. Is your family musical?"

"Oh, sure. We used to march around Switzerland singing about hills and goats all the time."

Darla snorted, sent Clifton a look, and mouthed, "She's deflecting."

He nodded. "Well if you get the sudden urge to yodel, warn us first, hmm?"

"Okay," Jessica said with a giggle.

Clifton leaned back into his seat. "My mom was a pianist at a small church. When my dad left, she supported us with piano lessons too."

Darla blinked several times. She wouldn't have guessed he came from such a modest background. "How old were you when he left?"

He paused, as if startled by her curiosity. "Five or six." His voice softened. "Mom was amazing when my older brother and I were young. She never complained. Never maligned my dad . . . not in front of us, at least. And she worked hard to provide for us."

Jessica seemed to read between the lines. "What about when you were older?"

Clifton sighed. "When I was twelve, we found out my dad had left us because he had another family. He'd already been married to another woman when he met my mom and he went back to her."

Jessica gave a little gasp that mirrored the indignant shock coursing through Darla.

Clifton continued. "Mom had overcome his leaving, but she couldn't deal with that. She sort of went into decline. She couldn't keep lesson appointments. Messed up at church until they asked her to resign. Things fell apart."

"She left too," Jessica mumbled.

"I guess she did, in a way. Not that I blame her, really. But it was tough for a few years."

Silence settled over them again. Darla adjusted her sunglasses and scanned either side of the road. There were honest-to-goodness bluebonnets blooming, but she couldn't fully appreciate the sight. Her mind was too full from Clifton's story.

"My mom checked out too."

Darla started at Jessica's abrupt declaration.

"She did?" Clifton's gentle prompt seemed to encourage the girl.

"Drinking," Jessica murmured. "She fought with it for years, went through lots of programs, but she couldn't get past it. When I was seven, she left me with my aunt in Texas and moved to Florida for a new job. In her emails and calls, she always says she wants me to come be with her just as soon as things get stable."

Clifton swallowed audibly. "And now they're stable? That's why you're headed down there?"

"Now it doesn't matter. She doesn't have to look after me because I can take care of myself."

Darla winced. *So grownup.* Sixteen or seventeen years old and ready to take on the world. Why hadn't Jessica just stayed with her aunt? Instead of asking, Darla simply said, "I'm sure she'll be thrilled to see you. I hope everything works out."

"I do too," Clifton concurred. "And it's nice having you along for the ride in the meantime."

12

Clifton couldn't help but notice that they had taken far fewer breaks when Darla was driving. Although he'd suggested stopping several times, she had waved the offers aside. Not that he could blame her. Who would want to quit driving a sweet Mustang like his?

But Darla may have paid for her enthusiasm, judging by her slow, laborious movements when she got out of the car in the town of Natchitoches, Louisiana, where they were stopping for the night. It made him ache just watching her, but by now, he knew better than to draw too much attention to her struggle.

Fortunately, the dearth of stops had allowed them to arrive in the early afternoon, which would give Darla plenty of time to rest before the next leg of the journey.

And Clifton could think of a lot worse places to rest. Their hotel was located in the middle of the beautiful old town's historic downtown area. Once they had checked in and unloaded their bags, they walked around the immediate vicinity. Jessica was instantly enamored with the quaint shops and centuries-old architecture, starting with the stately Minor Basilica of the Immaculate Conception, which stood next to their hotel. Noting her enthusiasm, Clifton suggested she run ahead and explore while he and Darla took a walk.

As Jessica practically skipped away, Darla watched, her expression gentle. Once again, he was struck by her obvious soft spot for young people.

49

"Clifton, I'm worried for her." Darla faced him. "She's so determined to be with her mom. But what if it's not even safe? What if her mom still has a drinking problem? What will that be like for Jessica? The next thing you know, she'll have to be the one looking out for her mom, instead of the other way around!" She waved an arm in frustration. "And we're taking her right to that mess! What if she ran away from her aunt just like you thought? What if—"

"Hey, hey, hey! Take it easy," he interjected. "One worry at a time, okay?"

A young family approached then, chattering and jostling around them on either side and drawing his attention to the fact that he and Darla were standing in the middle of a sidewalk.

"Look, why don't we walk?" he suggested.

They moved forward, but Darla winced and she appeared to be trying not to limp.

"Unless you'd rather sit?"

She looked down and a hint of color tinged her cheeks, as if she were embarrassed that he'd noticed her effort. "No, I really need to stretch out, if you don't mind walking at a snail's pace."

"Of course not." He offered her his arm then, which she frowned at so quickly that he was certain she would refuse. But after a pause, she wrapped her arm through his.

"Thanks."

Once they were going forward again, Clifton resumed the conversation. "I, for one, have been too pessimistic about all of this. Maybe she's not a runaway. Your friend is looking into it, right? We can only speculate in the meantime, and that's not helpful." He squeezed Darla's arm. "What if it all works out? This could be really good for Jessica and her mom. Their relationship is important, and if they're both willing to try, who knows what might come out of it?"

She pursed her lips, looked away, then returned her attention to him. Her expression turned enigmatic. He almost had the sense she was trying to puzzle him out just as much as he was her. Finally, she blew out a breath. "Yeah, I guess you're right. There's no sense in fretting about it until we have all the facts."

They continued in silence. But it wasn't the oppressive silence from when they had first started this trip. It was thoughtful, tranquil . . . harmonious even. After a moment, Darla startled him with a change of subject. "Did you ever communicate with your father again? After you found out about his other family, I mean."

"I saw him quite a few times, actually, around my last couple years of high school."

The memories weren't the gaping wounds they had once been. Now they were simply scars, and like many scars, they had their stories. "He decided that since I was grown, he needed to take an interest in shaping me. He wanted to help me get into the right colleges so I could go to law school one day. He said the most important thing a man could do was find a solid career and settle down to build a family."

"He said what?" Darla exclaimed, mouth agape.

"Yeah, I don't think he appreciated the irony of that advice as much as I did."

"So what did you do?"

"The only thing I thought I could do. I studied architecture the way I'd always wanted to. When I got out, I worked until I was able to get my own business, traveling for projects and *not* settling down."

Darla actually threw her head back and laughed. "Of course! What else could you do?"

He warmed at the sight of her amusement, her understanding of his situation. And he laughed with her.

When they were quiet again, she said. "You did have a family, though."

A dull ache began to throb inside him. "Yes. I still wanted a family. I wanted people around me who cared about me and who I could take care of, even if it wasn't always the way everybody else does it. When I met Cindy, she seemed to go along with those dreams. We were young. It was an adventure. And it was still an adventure when Ashley came along.

"Ashley saw so many things: Niagara, the Grand Canyon, and lots of places in between. She got out and explored more of her world before she was ten years old than some workaholic bores see by the time they're middle-aged!"

Darla's arm tensed, and he glanced over to see a scowl settle on her face.

Looking away, he replayed his last words in his head. Then he mentally smacked himself when he realized how she'd probably construed them. "No! I didn't mean you," he rushed to assure her.

He snagged another glance at her face and was shocked to see, not the expected irritation, but vulnerability.

Pressing her arm, he mustered all the sincerity he possessed. "You're a lot of things, Darla, but a bore is certainly not one of them."

She responded with a tiny grin. "Ah, well, that's news to me, but thank you."

They edged away from the street to let another couple pass, then Darla spoke again. "It sounds like things were going well for you back then."

His shoulders threatened to sag, but he forced himself to stand tall since Darla was leaning on his arm. "Things *were* going well. But then the worst thing happened: they started growing up."

Darla shifted toward him. "They?"

"Cindy said it was time for Ashley to settle down and have some stability. Frankly, I think she was ready for it too."

"But you weren't?"

"No, but I did try. Staying put really didn't fit my business model so I went to work for another firm."

They slowed as they approached a bench and he gestured toward it. "Wanna rest a minute?"

She nodded and once they were seated, he continued. "We made it okay for a couple of years, but I didn't have the success I'd had before. That was an issue. Finally, we just called it quits. I went back to what I was doing, and Cindy and I kept a good relationship after that. And I still tried to give my girl her adventures. I wasn't about to lose her."

A mirthless laugh escaped his throat. "Only I did lose her."

Darla's voice was low and softer than he'd ever heard it as she asked, "What happened?"

"An accident. Ashley was riding her bicycle near a busy roadway and fell into traffic."

Darla gasped. "Oh my word. W-were you around when it happened?"

"No. I was on a job, as usual. I didn't even see her afterwards."

"You didn't see . . . her?"

"Her body," he snapped. Even the word felt empty and cold on his tongue. "Cindy had her cremated before I got there."

"What?" Darla's tone turned irate. "Before you saw her? Did you agree to that?"

"Absolutely not. I was furious on top of everything else, but Cindy said she thought it was for the best."

The memory of Cindy's action used to infuriate him, but today, he only felt an odd chill, notwithstanding the pervasive afternoon heat. Absently, he stretched out his legs in the sunlight.

Darla stirred and he turned to see her staring at the ground. "Clifton, I had no idea. I knew you'd lost a child, but Lucinda never told me the details." She raised her head and met his eyes, her own thoughtful and grave. "You must have been shattered."

"I—I was, yes." It was strange to talk about it. He almost never did. "At first, it was the worst kind of nightmare. I didn't think I could bear it. But after some time passed, I don't know what happened. Maybe I did it to myself. Maybe I ran away, but I . . ." He hated to say it.

"Couldn't feel anything?"

He straightened and twisted to see Darla better. How did she know?

"That's right," he admitted. "In some ways, I thought that was better, but after three years . . ." he bit his tongue. Why did he have to carry on so? He rubbed his hand over his face. Darla didn't need to know how long he'd been like this. Or maybe she did.

"Nothing makes a dent with me anymore: the stuff I used to enjoy, the work I loved. Things can go well or they can be a struggle. It's all the same. I just don't feel much. Even when I met Lucinda." He faced Darla completely now. "You need to know: I cared about your sister very much. Truly. She was such a kind and nurturing soul. How could I not? But I've felt like only half of a person for so long, and I didn't think she deserved to be tied to me like that."

"She wouldn't have minded."

"I know! But it still seemed wrong."

Darla watched him, unblinking for a second, and he squirmed.

"Right. So maybe it was also wrong to accept her affection when I didn't believe I should marry her. Maybe it was selfish to take when I gave so little."

When Darla didn't respond, he braced for one of her diatribes, but her cell phone started ringing instead.

Frowning, she dug in her purse and pulled out her phone to look at the screen. Her brow cleared. "I better take this."

"Gary, hi," she answered. "You did? Good."

Clifton scooted to the edge of the bench, as it dawned on him that the call was probably about Jessica.

Darla continued to nod and give brief responses. "I see. Okay. No, no, I wouldn't expect you to do that anyway. But . . . oh!" Her eyes widened a bit. "You don't say. Well, thank you, Gary. You've been a big help. Okay, bye."

She dropped the phone back into her bag and looked at Clifton. "Jessica is not a runaway."

He sighed in relief. "That's great."

"My friend Gary did a little more research too. There are a lot of things you can't access for a minor, but he found a record to indicate she's emancipated."

"Oh, wow." Clifton chewed on that a little. "I think Jessica's been forthright with us."

Before Darla could respond, Jessica herself bounced down the street in their direction. They both stood as she approached.

"Guys, they have some of the cutest stores here! I found an old-fashioned candy store around the corner. Look! Fudge." She opened a white box and extended it to Darla.

"Who can turn down an offer like that?" Darla said, reaching inside for a piece. "Thank you, dear."

Clifton accepted the fudge Jessica offered him, and watched as Darla and the girl munched on the treat and praised it. He had the sense that, like him, Darla was more at ease now that they knew a little more of Jessica's situation.

Really, Darla had slowly grown more at ease in general over the last few days. But what if today's conversation had stymied that? What did she think of his selfishness now that she knew the extent of it? Did she think he was as weak as he thought himself? For just a moment, it seemed like they'd made progress toward something like friendship.

He stood back as Darla and Jessica joked, drawn in by the cheery sound of their laughter, like a freezing man watching a fireplace through a window. They *had* been making progress. And maybe it was more selfishness, but he wasn't ready to give up.

"Hey, I was thinking," he interjected, prompting them both to stop and look at him. "It's still early. Who's up for a field trip?"

13

If she were being honest, Darla *wasn't* up for a field trip. The day's drive, though short, had still been tiring and, more than anything, she felt a need to sit by herself for a while and process her conversation with Clifton. But when he'd explained that he wanted to take them to a nearby nature preserve, Jessica's eyes had lit up as she told them she'd never been to one. So that had been that.

Fortunately, walking the lush, iris-strewn trail at the Briarwood Nature Preserve was quiet and peaceful, as field trips went. Neither Clifton nor Jessica seemed to expect her to talk much at the moment. They had walked a few feet ahead and were standing at the base of a pine tree, looking up. Darla looked up too and gasped. The tree seemed to reach up all the way into the puffy white clouds above.

"This is the oldest longleaf pine in Louisiana," Clifton told Jessica. "It's around 450 years old."

"Whoa!" Jessica's mouth dropped open.

"Yeah! Even *I'm* just a baby in comparison," Clifton quipped.

Darla snickered under her breath, and moved away from the tree toward another cluster of deep purple irises, but her focus remained on Jessica and Clifton.

It occurred to Darla that Clifton's interaction with the girl was probably very similar to how he'd behaved with his own daughter.

Darla's stomach contracted as his story about the teenager's accident replayed in her head. *So sudden and heartbreaking.* She'd almost told him how well she understood, but she hadn't. That memory had been all but locked away for almost thirty years and it was best it stayed that way.

But Clifton had lost his only child. There was no way he could lock that reality away, so he'd dealt with it as well as he could.

Darla turned her back to the others, feigning interest in another pine tree to hide the surprising tears that blurred the edges of her vision. Clifton's loss had taken an enormous toll; so much that he seemed to think he was incomplete and broken now. And in all of her hasty assumptions—presumptions, really—all of her harsh judgments, she never would have dreamed that this sense of brokenness had kept Clifton from committing to her sister. He hadn't owed Darla an explanation, but he'd offered it anyway. It was just one of the many proof points stacking up to show that Clifton Peters was an entirely different man than she'd thought him to be.

"Wait, look!" Jessica cried out. "Careful, Clifton, don't scare it away."

"Hey, isn't he something?" Clifton replied. "I think this is a specimen for Discovery-Channel Darla."

Darla turned and quirked a brow at the moniker. Lucinda must have told him about her fondness for animal documentaries.

Clifton beckoned her over, and when she walked nearer, she found Jessica crouched on the ground looking at a tiny shell.

Darla bent down for a better look. "It's a diamondback terrapin!"

"Look, he's poking his head out! He's sooo cute!" Jessica squealed.

Darla couldn't help but laugh at the girl's delight, and she glanced over to see Clifton smiling too. Their gazes met, and his smile widened until it crinkled the tiny lines around his eyes. For some reason, it became difficult for Darla to look away.

"Oh, he went back in his shell," Jessica reported, reclaiming their attention.

"Sounds tempting," Darla muttered.

"Huh?" The girl looked up.

"Nothing," Darla said. "We'd better keep moving. They'll probably be closing before long."

As they finished their walk, Darla pointed out a few of the migratory birds she recognized. When they spotted the bright yellow head and blue feathers of a prothonotary warbler in the hollow of a tree, Darla shared a few of the details she remembered from one of her favorite bird documentaries. Like the kids back in New York always did, Jessica giggled through descriptions of breeding habits. But, after a moment, she sobered and said, "Would people be happier if their relationships were more like birds?"

"You mean if people fed their kids worms?" Clifton asked, eyes exaggeratedly wide.

Jessica rolled her eyes. "No! What if, instead of aiming for happily-ever-after stuff, people picked partners for a time period while it made sense, like some birds have one mate during breeding season and then move on to another next time?"

Clifton laughed. "I think plenty of people do that already, whether they realize it or not."

"And some people never bother to pick one in any season," Darla remarked.

Jessica sighed. "Yeah, I guess people are a lot more complicated than birds." She shuffled forward, then paused. "Have you ever been married, Darla?"

"Nope."

"Did you even think about it?"

Darla balked. How did they get on her life? She rubbed her head and peeked at Clifton between her fingers. He seemed to be watching for her response, even as he kept part of his focus on the trail ahead of them.

She heaved a resigned sigh. After prodding both Clifton and Jessica for personal details over the last couple of days, it wouldn't be fair to demand the privilege of being completely closed off.

"I was engaged not long after law school."

"Really?" Jessica prompted, kicking a tree branch out of her way with an enthusiasm that matched her tone.

"Yes. His name was Raymond. Not 'Ray,' mind you. Raymond." She shook her head. After all these years, she could still hear his officious voice in her mind. "We were two of a kind: both equally committed to building our careers. He was in real estate law while my focus was corporate."

"So you had stuff in common. That's good, right? What happened?"

Darla paused and leaned down to stroke the petals of one particularly exquisite mauve-colored iris. *So delicate.* She straightened and regarded Jessica. "I guess you might say *life* happened. I lost my younger brother very suddenly.

"Lucinda, Jeffrey, and I were about as different as three siblings could be, but we'd always been close. When Jeffrey died, I—" Her throat tightened unexpectedly, so she cleared it. "I had a hard time getting over it. In fact, I had a bit of a breakdown. After a month or two, Raymond couldn't understand why I couldn't snap out of it. He didn't know how to deal with me, so he broke things off. Said if every setback was going to create that much drama then we probably weren't compatible."

They shuffled along for a few minutes with no sounds but the rustle of their footsteps. Darla's thoughts wandered backward from the memory. Raymond asking for his ring back right after she'd quit her first law firm job because she couldn't focus properly. The weeks of struggle that led to her quitting. Jeffrey's funeral. Then before that . . . No! She wouldn't go there today.

Turning to her right, she was taken aback to see Jessica's brow knit in a deep scowl. Curious, she looked at Clifton next. His jaw was clenched. What had she said to make them both angry?

"That's it?" Jessica finally blurted out. "The dude ran off because you were *grieving?*"

"I guess you could say that, yes." Although she'd been hurt, Raymond's leaving hadn't seemed as bizarre to her as Jessica apparently thought it was. Darla and her crisis had become a liability to Raymond's ambitions. She'd cared about him enough not to want to hold him back, so she'd accepted his choice.

"He was busy. He had a lot of goals," Darla attempted to explain.

"And you were an inconvenience!" Clifton's interruption was almost a growl. "What kind of man leaves a partner during something like that?"

Darla stared at Clifton. Her thoughts turned to a late-night memory of him bending over Lucinda's bed and holding her upright to drink some water once she'd grown too weak to hold the glass herself. What kind of man? Certainly not a man like Clifton.

He shoved his hands in his pockets. "Oh, I'm sorry to carry on, Darla. You probably don't want to rehash all of that."

"I'm sorry too," Jessica rushed to agree. "I shouldn't have brought it up."

Darla waved a dismissive hand. "It's fine. That was a long time ago. It worked out better for both of us."

"Oh, yeah?" Clifton's voice held a note of sarcasm. "I guess he found a nice girl? One unencumbered with human emotions, perhaps?"

Jessica snorted.

"Ooh, let me guess," Clifton continued, "he married a mannequin from Bergdorf's, right?"

"No!" Jessica held up a finger. "I'll bet he built a girl in his basement."

Clifton guffawed loud enough to scare all of the terrapins in the preserve.

"Oh, you guys are too much!" Darla exclaimed with a sternness that even she knew was unconvincing, especially since in the next second, she was doubled over with laughter too.

They made their way back to the car, only stopping once more to marvel at a swarm of butterflies that materialized around them, as if drawn to their merriment.

14

"Come on, try it. Try it!" Clifton urged before looking down to realize he was practically bouncing on the balls of his feet.

"Can you at least let us sit down first?" Darla asked with a roll of her eyes.

But there was no real rancor in her voice. Just the teasing, good-natured crankiness he was finally recognizing as part of her sense of humor.

He shifted the bag of food he was holding from his right hand to his left so he could point better. "Okay, okay. There are a couple of benches over there. Let's sit down."

Darla and Jessica headed in the direction he'd indicated.

After their lengthy excursion to the preserve, they'd collectively decided to grab a to-go dinner instead of going to a sit-down restaurant. On their way back, they'd stopped for some famous Natchitoches meat pies, and now they were getting ready to eat them outdoors near their hotel.

Clifton had favorite haunts and cuisine in almost every town he passed through when traveling. In these last couple of years, before he'd stopped working, anyway, frequenting these places had become less of a pleasure and more of a ritual—just something he did because he always had. But tonight, he had the opportunity to introduce Jessica and Darla to one of his favorite things, and he was genuinely excited.

Once they were all seated, Darla and Jessica opened their boxes. Darla removed the large, golden brown, half-moon shaped pie from its wrapper and examined it.

"Doesn't that look heavenly?" he asked.

"Sure. If heaven is eating a whole week's worth of calories in one sitting."

"Oh, come on, Darla. Would you just try it before it gets cold? Have you ever *carpe diem*-ed in your life?" he needled her.

Ignoring their banter, Jessica took a big bite of her meat pie. Clifton turned his attention to her as she chewed.

Jessica closed her eyes. "Oh, my gosh, guys, this is sooo good!"

Clifton grinned. "Isn't it?"

"Yes! The crust is so flaky and warm, and the filling! It's like a whole meaty banquet in a little pocket. Yum."

"That's quite a review," Darla conceded. "I guess I'll have to give this a try." She took a bite and chewed slowly. "Hmm. Interesting . . ."

"Well?" he asked.

Instead of responding, she took another deliberate bite. "Very interesting . . ."

"Darla!"

She swallowed and her face lit up. "All right, I give up! It's amazing," she laughed.

"Yes!" he raised his fist. Then he started in on his own pie. The crust practically melted on his tongue, then there was a burst of hearty meat and spice. "Wow, this is good."

Jessica's eyebrows went up. "Yeah, but didn't you say you've had these lots of times?"

"I have, but I don't know. They just seem especially good tonight."

He glanced at Darla and found her scrutinizing him. He sent her a shrug and kept eating.

It didn't take long for them to finish their meal, but they were all three reluctant to get up and go inside. Maybe it was the mild, balmy night air or fatigue from the day's activities, or maybe it was carb-induced inertia. But whatever it was, it caused them to stay and keep chatting.

They passed through several topics before Jessica murmured, "Darla, I really am sorry about prying into your business earlier."

Darla patted the girl's arm. "It's okay. I mean it."

"Yeah, but I hope I didn't upset you with the bad memories, especially about your brother. I sort of understand why that's hard."

Clifton and Darla both shifted to watch the girl. "Is that right?" Darla asked. "Did you lose a sibling?"

"No, not that. But a few years ago, my best friend died."

Clifton's breath escaped in a whoosh. This girl had been through so much in her short life.

Darla gave Jessica's arm another pat. "I'm so sorry. Was she sick?"

Jessica crossed her arms and hunched forward. "No. It was a drug overdose." She began to rock back and forth slightly. "I was the one who found her."

Darla's eyes squeezed shut. When she opened them, she exchanged a pained look with Clifton. She continued to rub Jessica's arm. "That must have been so hard."

Jessica nodded. "That part was bad, yeah. But mostly, I just miss her. We weren't friends all that long, but we just connected and understood each other." She reached into her backpack and pulled out a thin, five-by-seven photo album. Flipping it open, she murmured, "This is her. Her mom took this when she drove us to a party one day, and she printed off a copy for me."

Darla took the photo and tilted it so the nearest streetlight could illuminate it.

The image flickered and Clifton's heart nearly stopped. Blinking several times, he leaned closer. What was the matter with him? Was he seeing things now?

Without noticing his response, Darla passed the picture to Clifton so he could see it. Once it was in his hands, his doubts vanished. *No. No, it couldn't be.* There was no way. He clasped the album until it wrinkled.

"Clifton?" Darla's eyes widened in alarm, as she studied his face. "Clifton, what's the matter?"

"My daughter," he managed to croak out. "This is my daughter Ashley."

"What?" Jessica jumped off the bench.

He scrambled to his feet too and shook the album. "What did you mean by an overdose?" he shouted. "That's not what happened to her. She was in an accident!"

"Y-yes, I always believed it was an accident. She'd just been experimenting for a little while, I think. She didn't know how much was too much."

His heart pounded furiously, and he stepped forward and snatched Jessica's wrist. "Experimenting? You're lying! She wasn't doing that."

"Clifton, let go of her this instant." Darla's sharp voice penetrated his spinning thoughts. She was standing beside them now, pulling on his arm. He blinked and looked at Jessica.

Her eyes were glazed over with tears and alarm.

Immediately, he released his grip and backed up.

"Clifton, Jessica, why don't you both sit down?" Darla said.

She half-pushed and half-guided Clifton toward the bench. Once the back of his knees hit the wooden slat, he sank down.

She helped Jessica to her seat next. "Now, Jessica, just to be clear: your friend was Ashley Peters?"

"Yes," Jessica whispered.

"And you know for a fact that she died of a drug overdose?"

The girl nodded. Her attention remained on Clifton. "I'm so sorry. I had no idea who you were. Sh-she talked about you, but I never saw you or your picture or anything. And I never would have brought it up like this, if I'd known."

Try as he might, he couldn't seem to process her words. His breath came in short spasms. Answers. He needed answers now.

Before Jessica could say anything else, he leapt to his feet and stalked away, only vaguely aware of Darla's nearly frantic voice calling after him.

15

Darla helped Jessica to the hotel room and straight to the bathroom. If she hadn't already had a few encounters with hysterical adolescent girls when working with the youth, she probably wouldn't have known what to do with Jessica in her present state. Ever since Clifton had stormed off, the girl had been shaking and sobbing.

Once they were in the bathroom, Darla turned the tap on cold and aided Jessica in splashing the water over her face. That seemed to soothe her fevered weeping enough that she could sit down calmly.

Then Darla fished her emergency stash of chamomile tea from her purse and brewed it with hot water in the room's coffee maker. Jessica obediently drank the tea and leaned back to rest on her bed.

"Darla, I didn't know," she murmured for the third or fourth time.

"Of course you didn't, dear. How could you?" She took the empty cup from Jessica and set it down on the nightstand. "Listen. There's nothing that can be done tonight, okay? So why don't you try to get some sleep?"

After a few minutes, exhaustion and the chamomile did their work, and Jessica drifted off, so Darla covered her with a blanket.

Then she went to a chair by the window and sat down. She looked at her hands and was startled to find them trembling. Clenching her fists, she stared out the window. When she and Jessica had come inside, they had passed Clifton pacing the sidewalk with his phone clutched to his ear.

Darla strained her eyes, but she couldn't see him or anyone else out there now. Where was he? Had he gone to his room? Was he still on the phone? Was he just wandering the streets somewhere? She clenched her fists again, then started tapping her fingers in an erratic rhythm on the arm of the chair. It was hard to imagine Clifton simply going to his room and to bed in the state he was in at the moment, so he was probably still outside.

Not that she could blame him. Her own head was spinning from the night's revelations, and she wasn't even connected to the situation. She could only imagine what Clifton must be feeling.

How was it possible that they had actually happened upon and picked up a hitchhiker who turned out to be friends with Clifton's daughter? And, if she was being forthright, which Darla was almost certain she was, Jessica was possibly one of the few people who could tell Clifton the painful truth about his daughter's death.

The whole thing was an unfathomable coincidence!

Immediately, her fingers stopped tapping and she winced. *No, not a coincidence.*

She stood and went to the closet where she'd stored her bags and found the one with her prayer book inside. Then she sat back down and read a few prayers and psalms. They always managed to quiet her thoughts. Afterwards, she shut her eyes.

Oh, Lord, what is this all about? I've been in such a state these last few weeks with Lucinda's illness and death. I haven't taken the time to talk or listen to you properly. And I guess it's showing. I've certainly fallen short on loving my neighbor where Clifton is concerned.

She sank further into her chair and groaned softly.

All I've done is look at him with judgment and suspicion. That's bad enough in itself, but now I see how wrong I was. Please forgive me and help me make things right with him.

She remained still for a few minutes, then leaned forward.

I don't just want to make things right. I want to help. I want to help Clifton and Jessica both, if I can. Is that why you brought me here?

Closing her eyes, she continued to pray until she slowly began to doze.

Suddenly, a soft rap on the door jostled her awake. She sent a quick glance toward Jessica to make sure she was still asleep, then stood and hurried to the door.

When she opened it, she found a tall man with thinning hair

standing in the hallway. He wore a necktie and a nametag.

"Good evening, Ms. Mayhew. My name is Mr. Walker. I'm the night manager here."

"How do you do? Is something wrong?"

His pale complexion flushed. "In a way, yes. The clerk who checked you in tells me you're traveling with Mr. Peters. Is that correct?"

Her stomach dropped, and she tripped forward. "That's right. Is he okay? Nothing happened, did it?"

Mr. Walker held up his hands. "No, no. I don't believe so. The night clerk did say Mr. Peters seemed upset when he passed by a little while ago, but that's not why I'm here. You see, Mr. Peters seems to be in his room playing his television set very loudly, and the other guests are complaining about the noise. We called his room and knocked on the door, but he didn't respond."

He straightened his tie and sent her an apologetic smile. "We were wondering if, perhaps, you might talk to him? This is highly unusual, but I could even give you a spare key. You all know each other, of course. Maybe he went to sleep or something, and you could wake him and ask that he keep the television at a more considerate volume?"

Darla's stomach was now a fine mess of knots. "Yes, yes of course." She accepted the key he offered. "Which way is his room?"

16

The horns in the late-night talk show band blared an upbeat tune as the camera swept over the applauding audience just before the show cut to commercial. Clifton gazed at the screen intently, listening to each actor-portrayed testimonial in the pharmaceutical commercial, and every item in the proceeding laundry list of potential side effects, as if he was watching a lecture in a language he only had a novice understanding of. Each phrase, each word, each musical note was loud enough to fill his ears without quite penetrating his brain. But that was okay. As long as he focused on the TV's roar, nothing else could reach his brain either, like the conversation he'd just had with his ex-wife. The moving images and sounds kept him suspended in a kind of electric haze.

The commercial break ended and the show returned with more music: horns, guitars, drums, pounding. Clifton squinted at the screen. Pounding?

Pulling his attention from the television, he looked at his door in time to hear the pounding again and see the door rattle with the force of the knock.

Shakily, he got to his feet and went to the door. "Yes?" he called.

The pounding repeated.

"Who is it?" he shouted.

"Clifton, it's Darla," her voice shouted back.

He squeezed his eyes shut. He wasn't ready to deal with Darla right now. Why was she here? Concern?

"The manager came and talked to me because people are complaining about the noise in your room."

Oh, that was it. She didn't want them getting kicked out of the hotel.

"Okay, sorry. I'll turn it down."

He grabbed the remote and turned the volume down a few notches. "There, I did it. Goodnight, Darla."

"Clifton! I can still hear it clear out here, and forget your 'goodnight.' I'm not going anywhere until you talk to me for a minute."

He settled his forehead on the door and growled. *Obstinate woman.*

"The manager gave me a key, and I'll use it if I have to."

But she didn't use it. She left him that last bit of autonomy. She'd probably give him more than that. She'd probably go away, if he asked her to sincerely.

"Open the door, Clifton." The words were framed like an order, but her tone was pleading.

He pulled in a slow, deep breath and released it with a groan. "Hang on."

He unlatched the door and pulled it open. Darla stood before him, her face wan and her brow furrowed as she took him in. He looked down, unable to recall if he was still wearing the same clothes he'd traveled in. Hmm. Same pants, but he'd changed from his oxford shirt to a t-shirt at some point.

"Can I come in?"

"Yeah, sorry." He stepped aside so she could enter, then he went back to the bed, scooting all the way to the back on one side and leaning against the headboard.

"Are you all right?" She took a halting step forward. "There . . . uh, there was some concern."

His forehead crinkled at her turn of phrase. "There was?"

She only nodded.

He got the feeling she was uncomfortable with this scene. It was best he do them both a favor and not draw things out. "I'm fine."

Picking up the remote, he turned the volume way down until the voices of the people on-screen were only a low murmur. "There. If you see the manager, would you mind telling him I'm sorry and I'll pay extra for the inconvenience?"

"I can do that."

"And I'm sorry he had to bother you."

Her only response was a shrug, as if it were unimportant.

He tossed the remote on the bed and stared at his hands. "How is Jessica?"

Darla took a few more steps forward. "She's okay. She's sleeping now."

"Good."

When she still didn't move to leave, he gave up trying to ignore the question in her eyes.

"I called my ex-wife Cindy and told her about Jessica and what she said."

Darla nodded her encouragement.

"She admitted that it was true. Ashley had been taking drugs. Cindy had only just started to suspect it when Ashley overdosed." He swallowed over the painful lump in his throat. "Cindy said the doctors believed it was accidental, just like Jessica thought."

Darla closed her eyes and shook her head once. "Why would Cindy lie to you about how Ashley died?"

"Why?" His temperature seemed to skyrocket in one instant. "Why?" he spat out. "You ought to be able to figure out the answer to that one! Cindy didn't think I could handle the facts because I'm just a man-child! I don't know how to settle down and be responsible, and I can't be expected to deal with the truth."

He shook his fist. "I ran off chasing my dreams, never giving a thought to the future; never seeing my daughter was growing up and . . . struggling with life. I never even noticed! And Ashley, sh-she didn't think she could trust me enough to tell me."

His throat closed up completely and his eyes started to sting. "She didn't think she could trust me, Darla. But I would have done anything! I would have moved back. I would have found her therapists, treatments—anything she needed, if she'd only told me."

"I'm sure you would have," Darla said, her voice quiet and soft. He looked up and saw that intensity that always seemed to surprise him spark to life in her eyes even though she wasn't looking at him. "But that's the kind of hell we humans get ourselves into sometimes. We sit alone, languishing in despair when all the while, love and comfort are just outside our door, if we'd only reach out and accept them."

She looked straight at him and moved closer still. "But, as hard as it will be to believe, you aren't to blame, Clifton."

He sat up and rubbed his head. "I don't understand you, Darla! I know you think I'm irresponsible and immature, and now when I'm trying to tell you you're right, you still want to argue with me?"

Her face colored. "I—I haven't thought any of that for . . . days now," she stammered. She looked down at the floor and shuffled her feet. "And I'm sorry for thinking it in the first place."

Clifton sank backwards slightly. That couldn't have been easy to say. And Darla's behavior toward him *had* softened considerably. It wasn't fair for him to gripe at her about how it used to be just because he felt like his world had just fallen apart for the second time in three years. She was here, trying to help him, despite not really wanting to be, most likely, and he needed to take pity on her.

"I'm sorry, Darla. Thank you for coming here. I'm not going to cause any more trouble tonight, I promise. And I don't think I'm up to talking anymore." There, he'd given her an out.

Instead of waiting for a response, he settled back further into the bed and returned his gaze to the television.

After a moment, there was a rustling sound on her side of the room, as Darla, no doubt, turned to leave.

But then he was startled by a clinking noise. His head jerked toward the nightstand on the other side of the bed, where Darla had apparently just removed her wristwatch and was setting it down.

To his growing consternation, she slipped off her shoes next. Then she sat down on the bed and scooted back against the headboard beside him.

Without another word, she folded her arms and started watching TV.

He opened his mouth to ask what she was doing, then closed it again. It wasn't that hard to figure out. She was just sitting with him, stubbornly refusing to let him be alone.

17

Darla's eyes popped open, and she squinted in the sunlight seeping through the partially open curtains. She started to pull up her blanket and turn over, but her blanket wasn't there. In fact, she was still in her clothes! Had she slept in them all night?

She must have dozed while sitting up, then settled into a more comfortable position during the night.

Gingerly, she pulled herself up. Then she froze.

Clifton was asleep beside her, snoring slightly and leaning semi-upright against the headboard with his head facing her direction.

At last, her memories from the night before returned one by one: the blowup at dinner, Jessica's tears, coming to see Clifton and sitting with him.

It had been the only thing she could think to do. She hadn't known what to say. He'd been so distraught. Even now, his forehead was puckered in a distressed grimace.

She had the strangest urge to reach over and smooth out the lines, but she didn't. She didn't want to wake him yet. Besides, she really ought to make her escape before seeing her in her early morning state gave him a heart attack.

Yet she couldn't bring herself to move. Instead, she continued to study his face. In some ways, it felt like the first time she'd really done so. Over the past few weeks, she'd seen his jaw tighten in frustration—often at something she'd said. But she'd also seen the lines around his eyes crinkle in laughter.

So why now, when she looked at him, did everything feel

different?

Suddenly, Clifton opened his eyes and blinked a few times before focusing on her.

Too late to escape now.

Even half-conscious, he was enough of a gentleman not to show horror at her appearance. In fact, he actually smiled.

"Good morning," he greeted, his voice husky from sleep.

"Good morning."

He shifted and stretched a little, then winced. Turning back to her, he asked, "Did we really just sleep sitting up like this all night?"

"You did. I must have, uh, reclined a little at some point," she finished awkwardly.

"That was smart." He twisted to look at her better. "How's your back?"

Even though his concern made her insides flutter slightly, she filled her voice with mock severity. "Excuse me, Mr. Spring Chicken. You were the one who sat up all night. Do you mean to say all your joints are in tip-top shape?"

"Not a one," he assured her with a smirk. "That's why I was asking how you were. I was hoping you felt like running to the store and getting me some Epsom salts."

They laughed for a minute then gradually fell silent.

Darla leaned over and touched her shoulder to his. "Are you going to be all right?"

The haunted look he'd worn when he'd opened his door the night before returned, and he didn't respond.

She said a silent prayer, then asked, "What about today, then? Are you going to be all right to face today?"

"I guess that's the best place to start, isn't it?"

"Yeah." She looked down at her hands and absently flexed the fingers that had gone numb overnight.

After another quiet pause, she felt him lean closer. "Darla?"

"Hmm?"

His tone was mellow and sincere. "Thank you for coming over here . . . for staying with me."

She continued to stare at her hands, but without really seeing them as she relived how she'd wondered and worried over him the night before. "I didn't want to leave you alone after everything," she murmured.

"I know. And that's why—" He stopped himself and stirred.

And then it happened.

He must have meant to move in and kiss her cheek, but she turned to face him in the same instant, and their lips brushed ever so slightly.

Her breath hitched in a faint gasp, and they both froze in place for several long seconds.

Warmth from his nearness began to wrap around her, along with a lingering hint of his spicy cologne. When he still didn't pull away, her pulse throbbed into overdrive.

It was nearly impossible to tell who moved first, but the next thing she knew, they were kissing. His lips explored hers gently and sweetly, and she found herself leaning in, even going so far as to reach up and graze the morning stubble on his jaw with her fingertips.

He released a tiny groan at her touch, and they abruptly pulled apart.

They were both a little out of breath as he leaned back and regarded her, his gray-blue eyes searching and intense.

"Darla?" he whispered.

"Yes?"

"D-do you think we could do this again sometime?"

She blinked and backed away. *Again?* Now that her senses were starting to return, she was a little surprised he hadn't run out the door after *this* time. "Um, I don't know if that's such a good idea."

He winced and turned his head. "Yeah, you're right. I'm sorry. Please forget all about it. I didn't mean to—"

"Clifton," she broke in.

"What?"

"I wasn't saying 'no.'"

His head swiveled to face her and he narrowed his eyes, but his mild annoyance couldn't compete with the grin playing across the corners of his mouth. "You know what?"

"No, what?"

"I think I'm all right to face the day now."

Her smile was quick and unforced. "I'm glad to hear that."

He picked up her hand then, pressed a quick kiss to it, and climbed to his feet.

****

When Darla got back to their room, Jessica was still fast asleep, which was a twofold relief. The girl needed rest after the emotional night she'd had. But not only that, Darla was glad that she wouldn't need to explain her absence. It wasn't that she had anything to be ashamed of, but it still could've made for an awkward conversation.

Darla slid into the bathroom to get ready for the day. After a quick shower, she stood in front of the mirror applying her makeup. Once she'd finished, she continued to stare at her reflection. No, she didn't feel shame at being in Clifton's room all night, as odd as that might sound to some, but her exact feelings about this morning were hard to make out. There was a mixture of trepidation and embarrassment, but why? Her only goal had been to make sure Clifton was okay, as any friend would.

Wait . . . were they friends now? It seemed like it from the way they'd laughed and chatted this morning.

But then they'd kissed.

To Darla's annoyance, the face reflected in the mirror began to redden.

Oh, for goodness sakes! It had just been a little kiss that had made things seem better after an epically bad night. There was no need to get goofy about it. She was a grown woman and then some, and she shouldn't let all of this detract from the fact that she had a mission now, just like she'd prayed about the night before. She wanted to help Clifton. That was all.

Squaring her shoulders, she pushed open the bathroom door, and stepped out.

Jessica was awake and sitting up on the side of her bed, strumming her guitar and singing.

Darla stood still to enjoy, although Jessica played so softly that it took her a moment to recognize the song as Fleetwood Mac's "Landslide."

How old *was* this kid?

Jessica paused her playing when she noticed Darla standing there, so Darla walked across the room to the chair she'd sat in the night before and pulled it closer to where the girl was sitting. "That was very nice."

"Thanks," Jessica replied, but her mouth remained set in a firm, sober line.

"How do you feel this morning?"

Jessica set her guitar back in its case. "Okay, I guess." She sat up straight and tucked her fingers beneath her knees and kicked her legs. It made her seem smaller since her feet didn't touch the floor. "Darla, this is all pretty weird, right?"

"What do you mean?"

"All of this: randomly meeting y'all and Clifton turning out to be Ashley's dad." Her head drooped. "And me being the one to tell him about what happened to Ashley."

"Yes, it is weird," Darla agreed.

Jessica looked up. "But what if it's not random? What if it was all meant to play out like this?"

Darla sat back and folded her arms. When working with kids in the past, she'd never been one to thump a Bible at them, but she also hadn't shied away from chatting about faith if they were interested. "It's funny you say that. I was just talking to God about that last night."

Jessica's face brightened. "Really? Did you come up with any answers?"

"No, not exactly. But it seems like it was important that Clifton find out the truth about what happened to Ashley. Even though it was hard for him to hear and hard for you to talk about."

"Yeah, maybe you're right." Jessica kept her head down. "Do you think he'll be able to deal with it?"

"I think so. And that was one conclusion I came to: I think maybe I'm here to help him with some of that."

Jessica looked up and a frown flitted across her face, but it was gone before Darla could even speculate on what had provoked it.

Jessica's expression returned to neutral when she said, "You know, lots of people believe God is in their corner and making things happen for them. I guess it's the 'all things work together for good' attitude. But then they get discouraged if they don't get the good things they were hoping for."

Darla nodded. "That can be hard to understand, yes."

"Right. But sometimes we forget that it's not all about us. I think about it a lot when I'm on the road seeing all the different people. God loves all of them the same, and his plan of love isn't just for me—one person—or one church or one town or even one country. Sometimes I think we just need to trust that plan more and ask how *we* can be the good working in someone else's life."

Darla blinked several times, taken aback by Jessica's insight. "I agree. We do forget to ask that sometimes."

Jessica giggled. "No, not you."

"Not me?"

She shook her head until her long hair cascaded over her shoulder. "No, I have a feeling you ask that question too much."

She giggled again and hopped off the bed. "You done in the bathroom?" Without waiting for a response, she dashed across the floor into the bathroom and shut the door.

Darla gaped after her. *Now what did she mean by that?*

****

Darla sent Jessica ahead of her to the nearby cafe where Clifton had agreed to meet them for breakfast while she finished packing her bags and ensuring the room was checkout-ready.

As Darla walked to the cafe, that odd mixture of embarrassment and nerves returned in anticipation of seeing Clifton again. But the feelings dissolved as soon as she arrived and found Clifton and Jessica deep in earnest conversation.

As Darla drew closer, she heard Clifton say, "Can you forgive a thoughtless old man?"

Jessica sent him a small smile. "You're not a thoughtless old man, Clifton, but I forgive you, and I understand."

He offered his hand for her to shake, and she accepted it. "I'm gra—" His voice was hoarse, so he coughed and tried again. "I'm grateful my daughter had you for a friend."

Darla hung back a second longer and swallowed over the lump in her own throat. When she was better composed, she approached the table.

As soon as he saw her, Clifton sprang to his feet and pulled out her chair. Darla accepted the gesture with a nervous chuckle. It wasn't unusual for him to pull out a chair for her and Jessica both, but he didn't normally pop up like a jack-in-the-box to do it.

Once she was seated, he passed her a cup of coffee, caressing her fingers just a bit in the process.

"Thanks," she mumbled and took a sip. Her eyes widened. Cream with no sugar, just the way she liked it. She met his gaze, and he flashed a grin she felt all the way down to her toes.

18

"Clearly, I've had too much coffee," Clifton told himself for the third time that morning as he stood at the back of his Mustang, furiously drumming his fingers on the trunk while he filled the gas tank. But the excuse sounded sillier every time he used it.

He was a twenty-four-ounce travel-coffee-mug kind of guy. The old reliable energy boost he normally got from his morning java was nothing like the live-wire, jittery feeling that had overtaken him ever since he'd kissed Darla.

He had kissed Darla!

This morning had been so surreal.

When waking up after a night like he'd had, he would have expected to be drained, disoriented, maybe even sick. But instead, he had stirred and found himself sitting beside Darla. Seeing her there had filled him with an inexplicable tranquility and . . . rightness.

Was that any reason to kiss her, though? He shook his head and carefully removed the gas nozzle from the tank before replacing it on the pump.

Honestly, he didn't know. It had just happened. But when it had, something inside him had jolted awake, as regard for the real Darla, who he was just beginning to understand, had fused with awareness of her nearness and warmth.

Now in the aftermath, he was left with an unfamiliar sensation of being excited and skittish all at once. Unfamiliar, but not wholly unrecognizable: it was the feeling of being alive.

He finished at the pump and did his quick, habitual inspection of the car. Then he went inside the station. When he'd asked if they wanted anything, Jessica had requested a tropical fruit juice he'd never heard of but was able to locate thanks to its colorful label, and Darla had asked for another coffee.

The long line at the checkout gave him a few more minutes alone with his thoughts.

His feelings were one thing, of course, but Darla's feelings were more important.

In the moment, she had seemed to enjoy the kiss as much as he had, but he'd worried she'd have regrets once they separated.

When he'd headed to breakfast, he'd promised himself two things: First, he would do his best to make peace with Jessica for his behavior the night before. And second, he would play things cool with Darla in case she needed space or was having misgivings about the sharp turn their relationship had taken.

His first goal had been more than successful, mostly thanks to the fact that Jessica was a sweet and good-natured kid.

But the second goal was another story. He couldn't help but act differently with Darla now. As soon as he'd seen her standing at the table, his heart rate had picked up like he was a junior high boy with a crush, and not a middle-aged man with more emotional baggage than he could fit in the trunks of half a dozen Mustangs.

Darla had always been hard to read, but what he could determine from her response to his nonsensical behavior at breakfast wasn't exactly encouraging. She'd seemed nervous around him too, but not in a good way.

Clifton's turn at the checkout finally came and he quickly paid for his drinks then stepped back into the mild but humid morning air. Back at the car, Jessica was still in the backseat, but Darla had gotten out, it seemed, for a last minute stretch.

He approached and handed her the coffee, careful this time not to make too much contact. She thanked him and took a drink. "Mmm. Perfect."

Then she raised an eyebrow at him. "I just want you to know that if remembering things like how coffee should be prepared is how you score points with the ladies . . . it's very effective."

With that, she got in the car and closed the door, leaving him laughing on the other side.

His nerves were a little bit calmer now.

****

Since it was about a four hundred-mile stretch from Natchitoches to Point Clear, Clifton had given Darla the choice of driving straight through or breaking it up into two days. She insisted she could make the whole trip in one day if they took an extended break along the way, so they stopped in Baton Rouge.

There was a plethora of things to do and see in the city, but Jessica's fascination with looking at the Mississippi River gave Darla the idea that they should visit the USS *Kidd*—a museum battleship.

Clifton found he enjoyed getting a peek into the chart room, bridge, and even galley of a World War II-era battleship just as much as Jessica did. Of all the sites and parks he'd visited with Ashley when she was young, he'd somehow missed this one. There was something exhilarating about seeing it with Darla and Jessica for the first time.

Once they'd finished the tour, they ate lunch at a bustling restaurant that specialized in po' boys and gumbo.

It was probably the combination of activity and a carb-heavy lunch that lulled Jessica to sleep not long after they were back on the road.

From her place in the front passenger's seat, Darla glanced over her shoulder at the sleeping girl and tittered. "Do you remember when you were young enough to be able to fall asleep anywhere?"

Clifton nodded. "Yeah, those were the days. But don't worry. If my granddad was any indication, we get another round of them once we hit seventy."

"Oh, good."

Darla reached down and turned the radio on to a low volume. The Beatles' "If I Fell" trickled from the speakers. They rode and listened in comfortable quiet for a few miles.

Eventually, he checked to make sure Jessica was still asleep, then said, "I'm not sure how much you heard this morning, but I want you to know I apologized to Jessica for the way I acted last night."

Darla reached over and squeezed his arm. "I'm glad you did that. I think she was worried over how it all played out."

"She's wise beyond her years."

"Mm-hmm," Darla agreed, "alarmingly so, sometimes."

"Ashley was the same way. By the time she was twelve, I couldn't get away with anything."

Darla scooted closer. "What was she like?"

He drew in a deep breath and released it slowly. "She was bright. Really bright, you know? I mean, she'd always been good at school and everything, but the last couple of years, as she became a teenager, she really started discovering how much she loved books. She'd go through so many in a week, it would make my head spin when I'd call and ask her to tell me about them."

"What was her favorite genre?"

"I think she was still exploring. She'd be reading Austen and Brontë one day and some new epic fantasy author the next. She was tenderhearted too. Everything affected her: sad movies, stray animals, books." His chest began to grow heavy. "I should have known how easy it would be for life to get to be too much for her and how it might make her try things she shouldn't. I should have paid more attention."

Darla's hand flew to his arm and settled there, firm and reassuring. "Clifton, don't."

He took his left hand from the wheel and placed it on hers. "How did you finally move past the grief, Darla, when your brother died?"

"Not in a very healthy way, I'm afraid." Slowly, she pulled her hand back. "I had quit my job not long before Raymond broke off our engagement. Once he was gone, I looked around one day and realized I had nothing. That's how it seemed, anyway. Lucinda was there for me, but I wouldn't let her in."

Clifton swallowed. Boy, didn't that sound familiar?

"So that's when I threw myself back into work. I got a job at another firm and later the legal department at a corporation. Everything that had to do with success and getting ahead was a battle then, and I ate that up, of course."

He looked over, and she sent him a wink.

"Of course," he echoed with a smirk.

"And that was my life for many years."

"When did it change?"

"Change?"

"Yeah. That's clearly not the case now," he pointed out, not insensible of the fact that, just a week ago, he'd thought that was the *exact* case.

"I got a wake up call. A literal one. I was diagnosed with thyroid cancer. It wasn't that serious, and the doctors were able to take care of it, but it made me think about how empty I'd let my life become. So I started going to church on a regular basis." She stopped and gave a short laugh. "You know what? I was actually arrogant enough to think, 'I'll hang out here a few weeks, get a few answers and some perspective, maybe, and go on with my life.'"

"But you didn't?"

"Well, I did get perspective. But I also got a few more questions in the bargain. But more than that, I discovered love: God's improbable love and acceptance for me and for all of us. That was the change, Clifton. Before long, I started wanting to know how to show his love. I sort of took a roundabout way of getting there, but that's how I ended up working with the kids."

"That's incredible," Clifton murmured, and he meant it.

Darla remained quiet for a little while. The shadows of the cypress trees they passed lengthened and reached across pockets of swampland.

He'd almost decided she must have dozed off too when she said, "Clifton, I'm sorry if I made you uncomfortable by asking you about Ashley."

"It's okay. I don't mind." Truthfully, in this moment, there was no one else he'd rather talk with about his daughter.

"Yes, but I should have been more sensitive. After all, there are some memories I doubt I'll ever want to share with anyone."

His whole frame jolted at that statement. Sharing or not sharing was her prerogative, of course, but there was a trace of finality in her tone that left him feeling cooler than the temperate sixty-degree evening warranted.

19

Darla hadn't been on a road trip since her twenties. Roads, cars, and people had all been different back then, but the most significant difference was how exhausted she found herself after a seven-hour drive. But this wasn't a normal road trip. It had already been mentally and emotionally draining for all three of them.

That shared fatigue was the main reason they decided to eat dinner at their hotel once they arrived in Point Clear, instead of venturing out into the surrounding area.

Although resources weren't an issue for her, Darla had originally been of the opinion that they should stay at a moderately priced hotel closer to Mobile, instead of a touristy, overrated resort.

Clifton had objected. If it was an option at all, he'd argued, how could anyone go to Point Clear and not stay at the beautiful, sprawling waterfront resort it was known for?

Now that they were here, she was glad she'd conceded that particular argument. Especially since the resort, though a popular tourist destination with its spa and the nearby golf course, was relatively quiet since they weren't staying during a high-traffic season. Dinner was a tranquil affair, graced with delicious local dishes, decorative piano music, and a lovely view of Mobile Bay.

After dinner, they took a brief walk, but the air was getting heavy with humidity and a cluster of clouds was moving in to obscure the moonlight.

Jessica went inside first to get ready for bed. Darla wondered if she sometimes took moments like this to call her mom and, perhaps, update her on the progress of her trip. But the girl never mentioned it, and Darla figured she'd done enough insensitive prying for one trip, so she hadn't asked.

Despite the thickening air, Darla and Clifton lingered outside a while longer. Clifton appeared to be scanning what could be seen of the various structures that composed the resort, probably analyzing the architecture that had evolved over the property's long, long history.

Her stomach fluttered a little as she watched him. There was no point in denying, at least to herself, that Clifton was a handsome man, especially when he was deep in thought like he was now.

As if he could read her mind, he abruptly looked at her and raised a brow. "Penny for your thoughts?"

Her face heated, but she laughed it off. "A penny? I never go for the lowball offers."

He chuckled at the remark and shrugged. "Okay, have it your way. But tell me one thing: you're glad we decided to stay here, right?"

"Yes, I am glad," she admitted.

"Not too touristy or overrated for ya?"

"Clifton?"

"What?"

"Have you ever heard of quitting while you're ahead?"

He held up his hands in an appeasing gesture. "Okay, okay. Sorry."

They walked in the quiet for a bit until Darla mused, "It's bittersweet being here, really."

"What do you mean?" They stopped walking and he reached down to brush one of her curls away from her eye, as if it were the most natural thing in the world.

She forced herself not to get distracted by the simple gesture. "When I used to come down here with Mama, Lucinda, and Jeffrey to visit my grandpa, we were pretty poor. Grandpa wasn't much better off, for that matter."

She gestured at the hotel. "This place wasn't quite like this then. It underwent some major renovations after the big '79 hurricane. But it was already the height of luxury in our eyes. I used to dream of growing up and making lots of money so I could treat our little family to a stay here."

Shaking her head at her childish fantasies, she pressed on, "Isn't that the way things go? Now that I can do all of that, they're all gone."

Clifton squeezed her shoulder and whispered, "I know."

He did. She knew he did.

She raised her chin. "But I'm glad Jessica is here."

His fond smile came swiftly. "I am too."

Then his smile turned arch and he took a half step forward. He was truly in her personal space now. "And me? Are you glad to be here with me?"

She swallowed once, and the heat came rushing back to her cheeks. Standing near him like this was doing funny things to her heart rate, and what's more, he probably knew it.

"Yes, but please try not to let it go to your head," she replied, and stepped away before she could get into any more trouble. "I think I'm about ready to turn in."

As she turned to go, he called out, "Good night, Darla!"

There was a bit of suppressed amusement in his voice.

She stopped in her tracks. Was he actually laughing at her discomposure?

Swiveling around, she looked him in the eyes. Even in the poor light, she could see the spark of challenge there, and she never backed away from a challenge.

In three deliberate strides, she was face to face with him once more. Close enough to hear his breath catch when she stretched up, laced her fingers into his hair, and pressed her lips to his.

After a long, breathless moment, she backed away. "Goodnight, Clifton."

"Mm-hmm," was all he could seem to manage in response. This time, he let her depart in peace.

20

Darla had only been in her room for a few moments when the sky crackled and unleashed a downpour. The wind picked up soon after, blowing the rain in sheets across the grass.

Her cellphone started ringing, so she grabbed it and looked in on Jessica to find she was already asleep. She quickly silenced the ringer and glanced at the screen to see Clifton's name. She stepped out onto her balcony. "Hello?"

"Darla, it's Clifton." His voice slid through her like melted butter.

"Yes, I know. I have you in my contacts."

He snorted at the remark in that same combination of irritation and amusement she often seemed to provoke in him.

When he didn't make further reply, she asked, "Was there something you needed?"

"I wanted to tell you it's raining."

"So I see, yes. Quite the little storm. I think we came inside just in time."

"Yeah, but it's nice watching it from the balcony. Are you standing on your balcony?"

"Yes, I am."

"Can you smell the clean, salty air? If you stand by the rail, the wind will blow droplets on your face."

The quiet awe in his tone compelled her, even though she couldn't make out his intent.

"It's almost like standing in the middle of a gulf wave right here on land. *I can feel it.*"

Her eyebrows lifted, as understanding filled her mind.

"I can feel it," he repeated, "and I-I just wanted you to know. Good night."

He ended the call.

She slowly sank into one of the balcony's wooden chairs and gazed out at the rain shower gusting all around.

I can feel it. His words reverberated in her mind and found their way to her heart, causing it to swell with gratitude and joy. Clifton was slowly healing, and she thanked God for it.

She'd been praying for Clifton a lot these last few days, just as fervently as she'd ever prayed for herself. In just a brief time, he had come to reside in that place reserved for the people she cared most about: her sister, Glenn, Natalie, and some of the kids she'd been working with the longest. These were her family and friends.

But Clifton wasn't a friend.

Her nerves started humming as she recalled the shameless way she'd marched up and kissed him less than an hour ago. She most certainly didn't behave that way with friends, or anyone else for that matter.

With a groan, she rested her elbow on the arm of the chair and leaned her head on the hand holding her cellphone. What in the world was happening to her?

Her phone gave a single, jarring buzz, and she looked at the screen to see a text from Natalie.

> **Natalie:** Darla, I haven't wanted to bother you, but could you please text or call, at some point, and let me know how you're doing?

Darla's heart filled with a fuzzy sensation. She should have checked in with Natalie before now, but she hadn't given consideration to the possibility that her friend would be that concerned.

> **Darla:** I'm sorry. Things have been hectic. Do you have time for a call now?

Instead of an answering text, Darla's phone began to ring a few seconds later. She tapped the screen to accept the call. "Natalie, how are you?"

"I'm fine, Darla, and so is Glenn. But how are you doing? How has the trip been?"

"Except for me having to stop so often, the drive has gone pretty well. We just arrived in Point Clear this evening. The plan is to scatter Lucinda's ashes in the morning."

"I'm sorry. That can't be easy."

"Thank you, dear. I'm sure it won't be, but it gives me peace knowing we're doing what she wanted."

"That makes sense. And what about you and Clifton?"

"What do you mean?" Darla asked too quickly.

Natalie replied with a short laugh. "I mean, how are you two getting along? You haven't killed or injured him yet?"

"Oh, that! No, no, I haven't. It . . . it hasn't been anything like I expected."

"I'm intrigued."

Darla had heard Natalie use that exact phrase and tone of voice after reading the first few lines of a new script. Only this story was stranger than any Darla had ever seen on a stage.

She settled deeper into the chair and gave Natalie a rundown of the whole trip up to that point. She didn't go too deeply into the details of Clifton's past; that wasn't her story to tell, but she did explain about meeting Jessica and most of the other events. The most glaring omission was her more demonstrative encounters with Clifton.

When Darla was finished, Natalie gave a low whistle. "That's unbelievable."

"Yeah, I'm having a tough time wrapping my mind around it all."

"I hope everything works out with the girl."

Darla shifted to look in the glass door behind her. Jessica still appeared to be sleeping. "I hope so too."

"Wow, but the bigger surprise is you and Clifton. I didn't doubt for a second that you'd be mature enough to get along with him while you needed to, but this sounds like a lot more than that. It sounds like you guys have gotten close."

Darla dropped her head back against the chair from the sheer exhaustion of trying to figure things out. "You want to know something else, Natalie?"

"What?"

"I kissed him."

Natalie's gasp was audible even through the speaker. "You did? My goodness, you have been busy."

Darla cringed. "This isn't funny."

"Sorry," she replied with a snicker. "But, seriously, this could be a good thing. It could be the beginning of a great relationship."

"I don't know about a relationship. I don't think that's what this is."

"No? Is Darla Mayhew a casual kisser? Who would have thought?"

"Natalie!" Darla pulled the phone away from her ear and glared at it.

"Okay, okay. I'll stop. But why are you so set against it? Why can't you just see how it plays out?"

"Well, I just don't think that's my function here. You'd have to be here to understand. See, when he called to tell me it was raining just now—"

"He called to tell you it was raining?"

Darla puffed out a breath. "Yeah."

"Had it been a while since you'd seen him in person?"

"A few minutes, but it's not like it sounds."

Natalie scoffed. "Really? Because it sounds a lot like a man looking for reasons to hear the sound of your voice."

Darla stood up and stuck her head out over the balcony to let the rain-soaked air cool her overheating face. When had she turned into such a blushing fool? Finally, she refocused on the phone. "Look, I understand how it might sound like that, but I don't think that's what is going on here. I want to help Clifton and Jessica, and I think that's why I'm in this situation. They've been through so much."

"And what about you?"

"What about me?"

"You're grieving too. Couldn't this be just as much about you? And what about this thing with Clifton?"

Darla squirmed and tried to interrupt, but Natalie kept going. "You two could have a real connection. Maybe God brought you together."

Darla had taken to pacing the balcony, but she came to a halt at Natalie's last statement. "It's nice to know you've become such an expert on God's plan in just a few months."

The phone speaker went completely silent, and Darla instantly cringed in regret. "Natalie, I—"

"No, you're right," Natalie mumbled. "I'm sorry for butting in, and I'm glad you're doing okay. I'll talk to you later."

She ended the call.

Darla threw her phone on the chair. What was the matter with her? She'd had absolutely no reason to talk to Natalie like that. For a second, she considered snatching up the phone again and calling back to apologize, but she didn't. At this rate, she'd probably only make things worse.

21

Clifton waited in the near darkness of the cool, clear morning, breathing in the salty bay air and listening to the rhythmic sound of the water beating against the pier. Before they'd started the trip, he had contacted Miles, an old friend he'd once worked with on a building project and who had retired down here, and told him what he and Darla needed to do. Miles had graciously chartered a twenty-six-foot panga boat on Clifton's behalf, along with a discrete guide to pilot it.

Miles had done well. The boat and pilot were ready and waiting to meet Clifton at the pier just after six that morning. The day before, Clifton and Darla had agreed that the pier would be their meeting place also.

For a moment, he considered texting Darla to see if she was on her way, but just as that idea flitted through his mind, he caught sight of her approaching the pier. She held the bamboo box in both hands. Just behind her, Jessica was walking and carrying her guitar case. He felt the corners of his mouth lift in an appreciative smile.

He and Darla had agreed that she would invite Jessica to accompany them on the boat ride. Neither of them would have blamed her for declining, but it somehow felt wrong to exclude her. It wasn't as if she was a stranger.

Moving forward, he helped Jessica onto the boat and then turned to take Darla's arm. As he did, he studied her face to try and gauge how she was dealing with the day. For the most part, her expression was neutral, but there was a flicker of uneasiness in her eyes.

He squeezed her arm. "Are you okay?"

"Fine, thanks."

"This is probably the wrong time to ask this, but do you have any issues with boats or water?"

"Last time I checked, no."

"Good. If you do, there is some medicine for seasickness on the boat."

Darla's eyebrows lifted. "Really? They think of everything, don't they?"

He looked away. "Yeah, uh, it's my medicine. I get seasick, so I took some already."

A startled chuckle escaped her, but she quickly coughed to cover it. "I hope it works for you."

"I'm sure it will."

After that, he helped her to a seat on the boat and took one close by. When Darla looked over at him as they started to move, she smiled. The uneasiness seemed to be gone now.

They spent most of the boat ride in silence. Thankfully, the motion and waves didn't bother his stomach enough to distract him from the breathtaking beauty of sliding through the bay right as the sun began to float over the horizon.

He glanced at Jessica, and her eyes were wide with wonder. Darla was more reserved, but he could tell she was taking in every sight and sound as well.

Once they were a good ways from land, the guide slowed the boat and lowered the anchor. The panga still pitched and rocked quite a bit, but it was manageable.

Darla carefully stood up on the port side of the boat. She looked out over the waters, now glistening in the golden half-light of the newly formed sun. "Lucinda . . ." She stopped, swallowed, and started again. "Lucinda, there's so much I should have said to you when I had the chance, even in those last couple of weeks. But when I woke up today, I wasn't thinking of those things. I was just thinking about all the people you and I had to say goodbye to: Daddy and Mama, Grandpa . . . Jeffrey."

Clifton's heart began to ache for Darla as he watched her lower her head and grip the side of the boat.

"I guess that means you're with them now. And I'm glad of

that. Family, community, relationships: they were everything to you, and now you have all of that beyond anything we could imagine here."

After that, Darla fell silent for a moment. Then she turned to Clifton and nodded, so he stepped up beside her and faced the water.

"Lu, you gave so much love to everyone, including me. Even when I didn't deserve it, and even when I didn't have much inside me to give back: you still loved. You taught me so much with that, and I want to try to follow your example with the time I have left."

He shifted and noticed Darla watching him but, this time, her expression was completely undecipherable. After a pause, she produced a kind smile. "Finished?"

"Finished."

She pulled her prayer book from her bag and proceeded to read.

> *Father of all, we pray to you for those we love, but see no longer:*
> *Grant them your peace; let light perpetual shine upon them; and, in*
> *your loving wisdom and almighty power, work in them the good*
> *purpose of your perfect will; through Jesus Christ our Lord. Amen.*

After their collective, "Amen," Darla looked toward the starboard side of the boat, where Jessica was seated. "Jessica, would you play something?"

Jessica inclined her head and pulled her guitar from its case. She strummed it thoughtfully for a second then started to play. Her clear voice drifted out over the water.

> *I am a poor wayfaring stranger*
> *Wanderin' through this world of woe*
> *But there's no sickness, no toil, no danger*
> *In that bright land to which I go*

Darla slowly sat back down, her eyes fixed on the girl as she sang. Clifton took a seat beside her.

> *I'm going home to see my Father*
> *I'm going home no more to roam*

I'm only goin' over Jordan
I'm just a goin' over home

I know dark clouds will gather 'round me
I know my way is rough and steep

Jessica's face brightened in a sweet smile that she turned on Clifton and Darla as she sang the next line:

But beauteous fields lie just before me
Where the redeemed their vigils keep.

Jessica closed her eyes. Her voice intensified and soared, and the tempo of her playing picked up.

I'm going home to see my Mother
She said she'd meet me when I come

The guitar's tempo built and built, like a pounding pulse. Then it halted. Jessica's fingers stilled, and her voice softened almost to a melodic whisper.

I'm only goin' over Jordan
I'm only goin' over home.

When the song ended, Jessica kept her eyes closed for a bit longer, as if she were praying or maybe even crying. Clifton reached his right hand up to wipe the moisture that had formed in his own eyes and was startled to feel pressure on his left hand. He looked down to find Darla's hand covering his. He raised his head and met her fathomless eyes, now swimming with several emotions.

A rustling sound on the other side of the boat broke their focus, and they moved apart and glanced toward the source of the sound in tandem. Jessica was returning her guitar to its case.

Darla stood up and crossed the deck. When she reached the other side, Jessica stood too. Darla placed her hands on the girl's shoulders. "M-my mama used to sing that song when we were little."

Then she pulled Jessica into a firm embrace.

Once she'd released Jessica and composed herself, Darla returned to her original spot and opened the bamboo box. Inside was another, thinner rectangular box. The funeral director had explained to them that it was made of a special biodegradable material.

Darla moved to the rail and dropped the box onto the water, where it bobbed and floated on the waves.

The sun continued its climb and deep blue overtook the sky as they watched the box drift farther and farther from the boat until it finally sank beneath the surface of the water.

22

Although she hadn't come right out and admitted it, Darla needed time to recuperate from the morning boat ride. To that end, she, Clifton, and Jessica had each gone in separate directions for the rest of the morning and most of the afternoon. Clifton had driven into Fairhope, the nearest town, and Jessica had gone off to find a good spot to read. Darla had rested in the room for a bit before venturing out to take a walk.

The finality of committing Lucinda's remains to the water had been more taxing than Darla had expected. It wasn't simple sadness or loss that weighed her down, though. She'd traversed an exhausting number of emotions. First, there was befuddlement at standing beside Clifton for this process in light of the odd shift their relationship had taken. Then there was tender appreciation for Clifton's words about Lucinda.

And there was Jessica's music, of course. When she'd asked Jessica to bring her guitar and sing, Darla never dreamed the girl would choose one of her mother's favorite songs. How was it possible for one song to strike her as beautiful and heart-wrenching, yet hopeful at the same time? It had been the perfect choice for that moment for many reasons, but it had left her with a longing to weep uncontrollably when she knew she wouldn't or couldn't.

Now that she was out walking around, she was plagued by yet one more emotion, although she'd have been loath to own up to it: irritation with her sister. All throughout the journey down here,

Darla had managed to suppress and ignore countless memories of road tripping with her mother and siblings when she was young. But now that she was actually here, she couldn't seem to do that anymore. That was probably exactly what Lucinda had intended.

As Darla walked the boardwalk and watched the water, the recollections floated back to her with the tide. Teaching Jeffrey to swim when he was five or six. Going fishing with Grandpa in his rickety old boat. Watching Grandpa and Mama boil crab behind his tiny, dilapidated house. The mental images filled her with forgotten contentment. If only things could have stayed the same.

She walked a bit more until she found her way to a small stretch of sand with a cluster of empty chairs, so she sat down. Reaching into her bag, she pulled out the envelope containing Lucinda's last wishes, which Mr. Palmer had given her after summarizing its contents the day of the memorial. She knew it was too thick to contain only one letter, but she hadn't bothered to open it until now.

Opening the letter, she reread Lucinda's request, then examined the envelope. It contained another item: a faded color photograph. She tilted the picture out of the shade of the hat she wore to see the image better.

It was a picture of her, Lucinda, and Jeffrey in their swimsuits standing in front of Grandpa's fishing boat. Darla was twenty-five, Lucinda was twenty-two, and Jeffrey was only sixteen.

"There you are."

She jumped at the sound of Clifton's voice. She must have looked pale or distressed because he hurried over and sat on a chair beside her. "Is something wrong?"

"No. I was just looking at this old picture Lucinda left along with the letter about her last wishes."

"Really?" He leaned closer to look. She hesitated for a second then handed it to him.

His face brightened. "Wow. This is you and Lucinda, right?"

"Yes," she tapped the photo, "and that was our brother Jeffrey."

Clifton's brow furrowed. "That's Jeffrey? But he looks like a teenager. I always got the impression from Lucinda that he was younger than that when he died. Not that she ever talked about it much."

Darla's stomach twisted. "She didn't?"

"No."

She guffawed humorlessly. "Well, that's perfect."

"What do you mean?"

"I was so determined to avoid discussing Jeffrey that I actually avoided Lucinda, and she wasn't talking about him either."

Clifton scooted to the edge of his seat until his knees nearly touched her chair. "What happened to him, Darla? And what really kept you away all those years?"

Darla looked in Clifton's eyes, so caring and concerned, and found she didn't have the strength to avoid it anymore. She brushed her fingers over his hand as she reclaimed the photo.

"This was taken just a couple of days before Jeffrey died. That summer, Mama's health had been going downhill and she hadn't had much time to keep an eye on Jeffrey. He started hanging out with some troublemakers, drinking, and doing stuff like that. So Lucinda decided it might be good for the three of us to come down here again like we always did when we were younger. I was reluctant to take time off from my new job, but it was very important to Lucinda, so I gave in.

"She had us do all the things we used to do when we'd visit, like fishing and swimming, but it wasn't the same. Mama wasn't well enough to come. Grandpa's mind wasn't as sharp as it used to be. I think Jeffrey wanted to leave almost as soon as we got here. Then he started drinking and causing mischief down here too. Lucinda was always big on getting him out of trouble, but I was more the tough-love type. I'm sure that's no surprise."

Clifton didn't laugh. Instead, he reached over and stroked her arm.

She continued. "One day, he got more unruly than usual, and one of my grandpa's neighbors called the police on him. They came out to arrest him and everything. Lucinda wanted to follow them to the station and bail him out right away, but I didn't."

Her throat went dry, and her hands started to tremble. "I thought a night or two in jail might scare him into cleaning up his act. As the police took him into their squad car . . . I told Jeffrey we weren't going to bail him out and that it was for his own good." A convulsive shudder ran through her body, and her voice came out like a whimper. "You should have seen the shock and hurt on his face, Clifton, but I steeled myself to it and watched the car drive away.

"But Jeffrey was drunk and upset. He wasn't thinking clearly. At the station, he hit one of the cops over the head and ran away. He ran all the way to the water, stole a boat, and wrecked it. It exploded on impact. Th-there was barely anything left of him to identify." Her hand went over her mouth. "That's why I had so much trouble getting over his death. It was the cold, bare truth I was trying to avoid: he died because of me. I killed him the same as if I'd wrecked that boat myself."

She closed her eyes tightly and struggled to steady her breath as she gradually became aware of her surroundings again. The water, the sand, the afternoon sun, and Clifton sitting beside her, listening to this horrible story. What did he think? Did he blame her like she blamed herself?

She ventured a glimpse of his face, but what she saw there stole her breath. His eyes were misty and filled with tenderness and understanding.

That's when it hit her. Clifton could relate to just about every feeling coursing through her right now: the grief, the guilt, and the deep, aching sorrow.

It was the closest she'd ever remembered feeling to any person in her entire life. And it was terrifying.

Quickly, she passed a shaky hand over her eyes. "So that's what happened. I guess you see why I haven't wanted to talk about it," she rambled. "I think we should go in now."

She jolted to her feet and started walking, but Clifton jumped up too, and caught up with her.

"Darla, look at me." He turned her to face him, one hand resting on each of her arms. "Look at me," he repeated.

She stared at the sand at their feet for a second longer then brought her gaze back up to meet his.

Leaning forward until their faces almost touched, he whispered, "Open the door, Darla." Then he pressed his lips to her forehead.

A shuddering sob broke free, and she practically threw herself against him. Immediately, his arms tightened around her, and he held her close. She couldn't stop the tears from flowing onto his shoulder.

"That's it," he spoke in her ear. "I've got you. Just let it out."

23

Clifton had no idea how long he and Darla stood by the water while he held her. Maybe it was moments. Maybe it was an hour. All he knew was that he would have gladly stayed like that for days, savoring the simple intimacy of needing and being needed.

But eventually, the embrace ended, and they moved apart—still holding hands, though, as if neither was willing to break the connection entirely. They strolled in the waning daylight, and Darla shared more memories.

It seemed that having the courage to tell that first, difficult story had liberated her to share a succession of stories, some happy and some painful. Each one revealed another piece of the personality and character of the woman beside him, and it was quite wonderful.

After they'd been walking for a few minutes, Darla stopped and sent him a smile that was almost shy. "You know, we could talk about some of your memories too, if you want."

He laughed. "I don't have the pressing need to make this about me right now."

Her smile faltered a bit, but she didn't pursue the matter.

He looked up at the darkening sky. "Besides, I think it's probably time we locate Jessica."

"You're right! She said she wanted to read outside, but I don't think she'll get much more of that done tonight without straining her eyes. Maybe she went back to the room."

"Maybe, but let's check someplace else first."

They walked for a while until they were at the boardwalk. Just ahead of them, a light, a couple of barstools, and a microphone were set up with a small crowd gathered around. A girl was sitting on one of the stools.

"Is that Jessica?" Darla asked.

"Looks like it," he confirmed. "Earlier, I noticed they were setting up a little open mic thing here on the boardwalk, so I thought she might have found it too."

Darla thumped his shoulder. "You're a regular Barnaby Jones about finding people out here, aren't you?"

"Barnaby Jones? If we're talking TV investigators, I'd say I'm much more the Magnum PI type."

She responded with a hearty laugh.

They joined the crowd then, just as Jessica was ending a song. The group applauded and whistled. Clearly, they wanted more.

When Jessica spotted Clifton and Darla, her eyes brightened. Then she adjusted the microphone and began to play again. It only took a moment to recognize the opening bars of "In My Life."

"She really is a Beatles fan," Clifton mumbled.

The melody and lyrics about remembrance and love floated over the crowd and burrowed their way inside him.

Darla scooted closer to him. Without taking her eyes off Jessica, she spoke close to his ear. "Please don't ignore your memories like I did, Clifton. No matter how much it hurts, bring them out."

Her mouth set in a determined line, and she turned those sharp, passionate brown eyes on him. "Reconcile with them, even if you can't be friends. Otherwise, you'll always be hiding from yourself."

Her expression eased into tenderness mingled with humor. "And I'd hate to see that happen to you. You have such a very nice self."

****

After returning to her room for the night, Darla said goodnight to Jessica and went to bed, but she didn't go to sleep right away. Instead, she turned on her bedside lamp and pulled out Lucinda's envelope again. She intended to look at the photograph once more, but this time, she noticed yet another item that she had failed to realize was in the envelope. It was a small note written in Lucinda's handwriting. Darla held it close to the lamp and read.

Darla,

I'm sure at some point, you've suspected this whole thing was an elaborate plan to force you to think about the past and what happened to Jeffrey.

Darla couldn't help but laugh at this. She'd mentally accused Lucinda of this very thing earlier that day.

And you would be partly right. Heaven knows you've avoided the topic and even me every time I brought it up. But it's okay. I understand. I didn't have that much to say on the matter, so I'm putting it here in hopes you won't ignore it now.

I know you're still carrying around guilt about Jeffrey, but please let it go. What happened to Jeffrey was tragic, but you couldn't control his actions. You did what you could. As for whatever mistakes you made, I'm begging you to give them over to God and find peace.

Love always,
Lucinda

Darla reread the note and sank back against her pillows. It was so brief and simple, yet so powerful.

Yes, she had been arrogant enough to think she could control Jeffrey's behavior. But that wasn't possible. People made mistakes; often harmful ones that their loved ones wished with all their might they could prevent. Her thoughts roved to Clifton. She'd encouraged him not to keep blaming himself. Could she take her own advice?

Slowly, she got out of the bed and knelt beside it.

Lord, I did make mistakes with Jeffrey, but I also tried to assume too much responsibility. The worst part is that I carried all of this around instead of giving it to you. Please forgive me for the wrong I did and the right I should have done, and help me find peace.

24

If there had ever been a morning in which Darla would have expected to sleep in, it would have been the day after saying a final goodbye to her only family and then practically having an emotional meltdown, the likes of which she hadn't given into in almost thirty years. But, as it happened, she awoke before dawn.

She sat up, stacked the plush down pillows against the headboard and reclined against them. Even though she was wide awake mentally, she still had the unusual sensation of being completely relaxed.

Or maybe it wasn't relaxation. Maybe it was relief that she was no longer actively avoiding an entire chapter of her life. Reliving those last few days of Jeffrey's life and her role in them had been difficult, to say the least, but it had also been freeing. It had freed her to ask for forgiveness and to try to move forward, Lord willing.

She could only hope that Clifton would find a way to move forward too.

Clifton.

Everything inside her seemed to glow as she remembered the way he'd held her while she wept. He'd been so sturdy yet gentle. She couldn't remember the last time anyone had been there for her like that. Of course, the better question might be, when was the last time she'd allowed someone to be there for her?

She shifted uneasily against her pillows. It was an unpleasant thought that she really didn't have the capacity to explore right this minute. Maybe it was best to save it for another day. Besides, she could only sit in bed for so long before her back started to cramp up. This would be a good time for a quiet walk outside.

Standing up, she gingerly did a few stretches, put on her bathrobe, and walked out of her room into the suite's spacious sitting area. Then she stepped back in surprise. Jessica was already sitting on the couch, fully dressed and tying her shoe.

"Well! I guess the worm goes to you this morning."

Jessica's head snapped up at Darla's statement. "Hey! Oh, I'm sorry. Did I wake you?"

"No, I didn't hear a sound. I just couldn't sleep. How about you?"

"Um, I went to bed so early last night, I guess I'd just had enough sleep." She gave a nervous giggle. "I thought I'd get up and walk or something."

"Yeah, I had a similar idea."

Something was off about the girl's behavior. Darla gave the room a onceover, and she noticed Jessica's backpack. It was packed, zipped, and sitting on the floor beside the sofa. That was strange; she didn't usually have her stuff together so soon after getting up.

"You know what?" Darla exclaimed. "Since we both had such good intentions, why don't we reward ourselves with room service? I'll bet this place sends up an amazing breakfast."

"O-okay, sure," Jessica haltingly agreed.

While Jessica looked at the menu, Darla sent off a quick text to Clifton.

Darla: I'm sorry to text you so early, but we're having room service delivered, if you want to join us.

A minute later, Clifton responded.

Clifton: Morning! That sounds great.

Darla: There's something else. I'm not sure, but I think Jessica was going to sneak out and leave this morning. But I got up before she could.

Clifton: Why would she sneak out? I thought we were going to drive her to Florida?

Darla: I don't know, but I think something is up.

Clifton: Okay. I'll be right over.

Clifton and the breakfast arrived around the same time, and they rearranged the balcony furniture so they could eat outside.

They chatted easily for a few minutes, but once there was a lull in the conversation, Jessica set down her fork and announced, "I think I'd like to go on to Pensacola today."

Darla and Clifton exchanged a look, but Clifton pleasantly replied, "If that's what you want, okay. We can drive you whenever you're ready to go."

Jessica waved her hand. "I can just take the bus. You guys have done too much for me already."

Clifton raised his voice. "Don't be sill—ow!" He glared at Darla for stomping on his foot then returned his attention to Jessica. "Err, anyway. It's only fifty miles or so. It's no inconvenience, and we'd be glad to do it. Really."

Darla leaned forward. "Yes, we'd be very glad. And, let's be frank, you must know there's no issue of obligation with us."

"Of course not!" Clifton agreed. "But I would feel better knowing you made it safely."

Jessica frowned down at the tablecloth. It was hard to tell if she was upset or indecisive.

"Come on, Jessica," Darla coaxed. "Just tell us your mom's address, and we'll take you there this morning. It's that simple."

Jessica looked up and scowled. It was the first time Darla could remember seeing her appear genuinely angry.

"Can I see your phone?" she asked Darla in a clipped tone.

"My phone? Well, sure. Hang on." Darla went inside to retrieve it and handed it over.

Jessica tapped on the screen to open the map application and rapidly typed something in the search box. When she was finished, she returned the phone to Darla, lips set in a firm, defiant line.

Once Darla saw the screen, her heart sank all the way down to her feet. Shakily, she showed the phone to Clifton, and his face sagged as he read the name aloud, "Barrancas National Cemetery."

25

Clifton stared at Jessica as she briefly explained about the liver failure that had claimed her mom's life at the age of forty.

"How long ago did this happen?" he asked.

"About a month ago. She'd recently married this guy she worked with, and he was the one who called to tell me she'd died and that he'd had her buried in the national cemetery. My mom served in the Air Force for several years when she was younger, so that made sense."

Jessica's voice had a sad, resigned quality. It sounded as if she'd forced herself to make peace with how she'd found out about her mom and the fact that she'd had no say in the final arrangements.

Clifton's stomach began to churn. He didn't know how to respond or even how to ask more questions. Darla was gravely silent as well.

Fortunately, Jessica didn't seem to need encouragement to talk, now that she'd started.

"I graduated high school a semester early. My plan was to go live with my mom in Florida after school."

"Weren't you happy with your aunt?" Clifton asked.

Jessica chewed her lip. "I'm grateful for all my aunt did. Really. If it weren't for her, I wouldn't have had anybody. But she took me in because she had to, and she never let me forget that."

"She treated you like an obligation," Darla muttered.

"Yeah, I guess you could say that. So even after Mom died, I knew I still wanted to get away. Florida seemed like a good place for a fresh start, and it would still feel like I was near my mom."

Darla's eyes met Clifton's then, and their expression mirrored his own distress.

Jessica sat up straighter. "I know y'all have thought I was being reckless and immature from the start, but I do have a plan. Besides my schoolwork, I went to night classes for bookkeeping and office administration training. There's a company in Pensacola where I can get a job right away, and I found a small, furnished room to rent. I even looked up some places where I can play music on the weekends."

She gazed out over the balcony at the morning sky and sighed. "I'm just ready to move on with my life."

No one spoke for several minutes after that, and nothing broke the silence except the occasional gull's cry. But finally, Darla said, "I'm so sorry for your loss, Jessica. And I want to apologize if we started out treating you like you were reckless or immature." She cast a glance at Clifton. "I don't think either of us thinks that's the case now, though."

"Not at all," Clifton agreed. "And I didn't mean to be patronizing when I said I wanted to make sure you made it to Pensacola safely. But the offer still stands."

Jessica's shoulders sagged, as if the conversation had worn her out. "Now that you know everything, I would like to ask one more favor then."

"Anything," he assured her.

"Would you drive me to visit my mom?"

****

Two hours later, Darla leaned against the Mustang beside Clifton at the cemetery while Jessica visited her mom's grave. Since the cemetery was on a naval base, Jessica's request that they drive her made perfect sense. Public visitation was allowed, but it had taken some red tape to accomplish.

They hadn't really spoken since parking the car and watching Jessica walk off, her guitar case in one hand and a bouquet of flowers in the other, but Clifton was the first to break the silence. "Is it just me, or do you think we should have seen this coming?"

Darla massaged her forehead. "No, I think so too. I just had my mind so made up about the way things were with Jessica that I didn't pay attention to the signs."

"Yeah." He rubbed the back of his neck. "I feel so bad for her."

Scooting closer, she put her arm through his. "So do I. It doesn't seem fair for a girl her age to have to deal with so much loss."

"I wish I could do something."

"I know you do, Clifton." She rubbed his arm and pressed a kiss to his shoulder because it seemed like the thing to do. "You want to swoop in and do the Papa Bear thing and take care of her; try to fix the problem. But there's something you have to understand. Something we both have to understand. Jessica is basically an adult. She thinks of herself and conducts herself as an adult. And she has the right to face her challenges in the way she chooses. Now, I think we should make sure she knows we're willing to help her if she needs it, but ultimately, she deserves the freedom to start her life."

He dipped his head with a sigh, and covered her hand with his, pressing it closer to his chest. "You're right, of course. I can't just march in and try to make things better for her. That isn't my place."

She could tell how hard it was for him to accept, so she decided not to belabor the issue anymore, opting instead to simply stand with him in the quiet.

When Jessica returned from her mom's grave, she was visibly upset but not hysterical. She accepted their offer to drive her to the place she planned on staying.

To Darla's relief, the furnished room Jessica had chosen seemed to be a decent sort of place, even if it was tiny. She and Clifton did what they could to help Jessica get settled in, but when they asked if she needed anything else, she replied that she only wanted to rest from the long trip and get everything in order before she started her new job.

As Darla watched Clifton give Jessica his phone number and email address—Darla had done the same thing earlier—it struck her as surreal to be saying goodbye to her in this fashion. In only a few days, it felt like she'd become an indispensable part of life.

Clifton forced a smile. "If you need anything at all, don't even think twice about calling me. Remember, it's not a burden. You were my little girl's best friend, and I won't forget that."

Jessica nodded solemnly. "Okay."

Darla stepped forward and wrapped Jessica in a tight hug.

"Take care of yourself, please, and stay in touch."
"I will, Darla. I appreciate everything."
And just like that, they left Jessica to start her new life.

26

Darla sat on her balcony the next morning, breathing in the moist, heavy air. The sharp blue of the sky was threaded with sweeping strands of cirrus clouds, and her eyes roved over them, tracing the patterns without really concentrating. Her mind was quieter than usual at the moment, and she idly wondered if she'd overtaxed it with all that had happened over the past few weeks.

As of the evening before, Clifton hadn't appeared to have reached that point yet. He'd been understandably listless and distracted during dinner and had excused himself directly afterwards. She hadn't heard anything from him since, but she tried not to fret over it.

A sudden tap on one side of her balcony rail startled her from her reverie and she stood up in alarm only to see Clifton standing on the other side.

"Morning!" he greeted energetically. "Did I scare you?"

"Oh no. Sometimes I just enjoy hopping up like a meerkat during breakfast. It's good for the circulation."

He snorted and shook his head at her. "Can I come in?"

"Of course."

A few moments later, he was perched on the edge of a chair on the balcony beside her.

"Coffee?" she offered, pointing toward the insulated carafe left over from her breakfast.

"Yes, please. I need it!"

She poured him a cup but stopped short of handing it over

when she noticed he was jiggling his knee as he sat. "It looks like you've had too much already."

"What?" He looked down. "Oh, I'm just keyed up. I was up all night."

"Why?" she asked, passing him the cup.

He took a swig and set the cup down with a thud. "Mostly because it occurred to me that I know a seventeen-year-old who has her future plans figured out better than I do."

Darla chuckled, but he continued. "So I decided I need to do something about that. Do you remember when I went into Fairhope the other day? Well, I went to have lunch with my buddy Miles."

"Oh, right. The one that chartered the boat for us."

"Yes. He told me that he's getting bored with retirement and wants to build a new restaurant down here by the water. He asked me to design it for him."

"Hey, that's great," she said, patting his arm.

Clifton's upbeat expression darkened. "I didn't think so at first. It's been so long since I worked on a project, and it was a struggle even then."

She nodded and kept her hand on his arm in hopes of being reassuring. He'd already explained how the numbness he'd been living with since his daughter's death had filtered into his creative abilities.

"But last night, I sat down and started playing with some ideas." He closed his eyes, and his features relaxed. "And it was different. The going was slow, but I could visualize again: windows, the façade, possible floor plans, and materials. I think God helped me find that spark again!" His eyes flew open and he jumped to his feet to pull a folded sheet of paper from his pocket. "I stayed up all night working out different visions, but I think this one is my favorite."

Darla stood up too and took the paper from his hand, but before examining it, she swept her gaze over his face again. His joy was so palpable that it made tears spring to her eyes.

Blinking rapidly, she turned her focus to the picture. It was a medium-sized structure. The image was black and white, but the texture of the walls suggested a wooden material like a beach shack might have. The windows were tall and wide, giving it an open-air quality, and there was a wide fire pit in the front with tables and chairs arranged around it.

"What do you think?" he asked eagerly.

"It's wonderful! It's like—" She struggled to find the words. "It's like a retreat from the rest of the world. Like a person could go there after a trying day and truly feel easy and tranquil."

His eyes crinkled in delight. "Yes! You see it, don't you? It's an encouraging start. This is a smaller project than I used to work on, but I feel like it's just what I need to get working again."

"I'm so happy for you." She impulsively hugged him.

His arms folded around and pulled her close. His embrace signaled comfort and heat all through her, like sitting by a fire pit on a late spring evening. He tilted his head and brought his lips near her ear. "Stay with me, Darla."

Her nerves thrilled at his words. Hope and excitement inflated inside her like a balloon. He was really asking her to stay? Did he really want a relationship with *her?* Notwithstanding all they'd shared these past few days, including the heartache, the healing, and the kisses, it seemed incredible. Amazing. And . . . unbelievable.

Pulling away from his grasp, she searched his face. "Are you serious?"

His brow furrowed. "Well, yes, if you want. You could stay with me here while I work on this new project, and it would be a good—you know—test run." He colored and laughed awkwardly. "I'm not good with words. I guess I'm just asking if you want to take a chance on this with me?"

A test run. Those were the right words all right, but her inner balloon snagged on them until the air began to seep out. She knew what she had to do.

She slowly backed away. "Things happened so unexpectedly between us that I haven't had much time to consider what it means or what it could mean for the future. The best way to figure it out would probably be a 'test run,' as you put it. But that's the problem."

Turning to lean on the balcony rail so that she was no longer facing him directly, she continued, "In business terms, I'm what you call 'risk-averse.' That's not a feature of my getting older; I've been that way for a long time now. I don't take chances when the outcome is uncertain. And with our history and issues, I'd say the outcome is more than uncertain: it's perilous."

"Darla, what exactly are you saying?"

She released a shaky sigh. "I'm saying that I'm sorry, Clifton. You're a good man, and I'm so grateful I got to know you, but I'm not ready to take that risk."

She ventured a glance in his direction. His shoulders sagged and his head drooped, but he didn't exactly seem shocked. "I understand, Darla. Believe me. I do."

Abruptly, he took a step forward, reached for her hand, and kissed it. "Thank you for everything. It's been a privilege getting to know you too."

Without another word, he swiveled around and left her standing alone.

27

"You wanna know how many people in the world died in plane crashes last year? Five hundred sixty."

Darla sent a sideways glance at the chatterbox sitting across the aisle from her and scowled. Why would anyone discuss airplane fatalities while actually flying on an airplane?

The talkative man's female companion gasped. "That's so many!"

"You think so? Now guess how many people died in car crashes worldwide?"

"Um . . ."

"I'll tell you. It was over a million!" he declared triumphantly. "So tell me again why we should have driven back to New York instead of flying."

Darla released a hollow chuckle under her breath. Now there was a man who thought about risk.

But what little humor the exchange brought soon fizzled out as she remembered her final big conversation with Clifton. He had offered her a chance for a relationship, and she had turned him down, using the excuse that she was risk-averse.

And she was. But it wasn't the risk to herself she was worried about; it was the risk to Clifton.

He had been a rock for her when she'd finally given way to grief after so many years of bottling it up. But that had only been the first step. She had a long way to go and a lot of issues to sort through.

121

To be sure, Clifton had his own past to sort through too, but he was already making obvious progress. His adorable excitement over his new project was ample proof of that.

He'd seemed excited, or at least sincere, when he'd asked her to stay too. But underneath that sincerity, she sensed his uneasiness. It wasn't hard to figure out that he was unsure about the success of their relationship, hence the whole test-run metaphor.

What if there came a day when dealing with her lingering problems interfered with his life or his work? Would he push it aside once again like he had for Lucinda? Was it fair to ask him to?

Clifton deserved the freedom to move ahead with his life. The possibility that she could be the one to interfere with that freedom was simply a risk she couldn't tolerate.

****

Clifton remained seated in his car in the airport's loading zone for several minutes after dropping Darla off.

Their goodbyes had been good-natured yet restrained, and they'd sort of rushed through them, as if she'd been late for her plane instead of two hours early. Some childish part of him had almost longed for their earlier antagonism. At least there had been feeling in that.

He sat reflecting on the incredible series of transitions their relationship had undergone, unwilling to start his engine and leave the airport, even though Darla was long gone by now. Leaning his head on his steering wheel, he indulged in a rare moment of self-pity.

She had left without promising to call, asking him to text, or making any other allusions to staying connected. That figured. Darla was too honest for pretense.

The angry blare of a car horn jarred him from his thoughts. He glanced in his rearview mirror and saw a car trying to pull into the loading zone behind him, but it was a tight fit. The man driving the car gestured wildly at Clifton.

"So much for Southern hospitality," he muttered. Waving a weary hand at the irate driver, he pulled away from the airport.

When he got back to his hotel room, he shoved aside the thoughts that had plagued him on the drive and sat down to work on the restaurant design.

After an hour, he leaned back to study the results of his labor and grunted. There wasn't anything particularly wrong with the floor plan he'd just laid out, but it was boring.

He threw down his pencil. Miles was entrusting him with his dream. This was a lousy way to live up to that.

A cool shiver ran over him from head to toe. Was he going to let Miles down? It seemed to be becoming a habit of his. Just like with Ashley. He'd failed her in the worst way by not being there when she'd needed help. She probably had no clue how much he loved her.

No wonder Darla had left. She knew the whole story of how he'd messed up as a husband and father. Why would she want to risk that? What had she said? "I'd say the outcome is more than uncertain: it's perilous." She sure had a cutting way with the truth.

He was a risk she just hadn't been ready to take. The words roiled and whirled in his mind like a gulf stream.

The wave must have carried him into oblivion for a bit, because the ding of his cellphone email alert jolted him upright.

Rubbing his eyes, he located his phone and opened the email application. Jessica's name popped up at the top of the message list.

He shook off the last of his drowsiness and opened the message.

Clifton,

I wanted to show you this last week, but it didn't seem like the right time. Maybe this isn't the right time either, but you deserve to see it.

-J

He scrolled to the end of the email, where there was a link to a short video clip. He tapped it and turned up his phone volume.

The words, "Jess's Heart Songs: Episode 1" filled the screen.

Jessica appeared next, but she looked to be several years younger. "Hey, guys! I'm Jess Connell and this is my first official episode of 'Jess's Heart Songs,' where I'm going to talk about music, play music, and sing music!" She giggled.

"But first, I want to introduce you to somebody special." Jessica disappeared from the frame, then returned pulling on another girl's sleeve.

Clifton nearly dropped his phone. *Ashley!*

Jessica put her arm around Ashley's shoulders. "Ashley is my best friend, and she's the one who talked me into making these videos, so I thought you guys should meet her. Ash, tell us all about yourself!"

Ashley laughingly rolled her eyes at the camera. "Ooh, that's not a vague question at all!"

"Okay, okay. Narrow it down. What did you do on spring break?"

Ashley's face lit up. "You won't believe this. My dad took me skiing in Colorado for the first few days, and then all the way to Myrtle Beach for the rest of the week!"

"No way! Your dad must be really fun."

"Yeah, he's the best!" Her voice turned bubbly and she began gesturing with her hands, the way she always used to when she was animated. "Every time we hang out, we go on a new adventure. But it's not like some busy dads where he's just trying to keep me entertained until the visit is over, you know? He actually likes to spend time with me." Her expression was sweetly content when she looked straight at the camera. "He really cares."

Clifton drew a sharp, almost painful intake of breath and paused the video on his daughter's beautiful smiling face.

When the tears came, he couldn't have stopped them if he tried.

Dear Lord, did she really know?

The rest of his prayer poured out wordlessly as he buried his head in his hands.

Long, long moments passed by until the daylight no longer streamed through his window.

And then he saw.

His eyes were squeezed shut, but the sight was so real he could almost touch it.

It was a bright, colorful garden. Butterflies and birds were fluttering around, and the wind was blowing through the flowers and grass. And there, kneeling down to tend or admire some of the flowers was Lucinda. After a moment, she stood and reached out her hand. When she did, his Ashley came running up to take it. The two of them laughed and strolled away, deeper into the garden until they were out of his view.

Slowly, he sank to his knees and his tears flowed freely on his clasped hands. *Thank you. Thank you, God.*

28

Darla paced the sidewalk outside the large gray building where Natalie was rehearsing and considered going back home. They often met up when Natalie was finished with play preparations for the day if they had supplies to buy for the youth group but, with no prior heads up that Darla was coming, there was a good chance Natalie would have plans this afternoon and no time to talk. Why hadn't Darla called first?

It was a silly question, of course. She didn't want to call Natalie because she'd been churlish and temperamental with her friend the last time they'd spoken, and it required a face-to-face apology. Provided Natalie even wanted to see her.

Just then, the building's glass doors swung open and people began to stream out, laughing and chattering. Natalie emerged with the rest and headed toward the street corner, but she halted when she saw Darla. "Darla! When did you get back?"

"Yesterday evening."

Natalie gave a subdued smile. "I'm glad you made it safely."

"Thanks. Do you have a minute or two to talk?"

Natalie glanced at her watch. "Yeah, I've got some time. I'm meeting Glenn later, but that's not for a few hours. Do you want to come with me back to my apartment? I can make us some coffee or tea or something."

Darla squared her shoulders, but kept her voice casual. "My place is closer, we can just go there, if it's okay."

Natalie's eyes widened. "Well, sure. That'll be okay."

Fifteen minutes later, Darla was boiling water for tea while Natalie sat on the living room sofa. She had the sense that Natalie was observing every detail of the room while pretending she wasn't.

A documentary narrator's voice filled Darla's mind. *And now we see the aging reptile in her natural habitat.*

Shaking off the thought, she poured up the tea and brought it into the living room. Natalie accepted hers with a thanks, then gestured around the room. "This is nice, Darla. It's very you."

Darla chortled. "I appreciate that. But now, for why I wanted to talk to you." She set her cup down and faced her friend. "Natalie, I'm sorry for what I said when we talked the other night. I was harsh and unkind, even by my standards, and all when you were being nothing but supportive. Can you forgive me?"

Natalie reached over and covered Darla's hand with her own. "It's okay, Darla. You were upset. You've had so much to deal with lately."

Darla squeezed Natalie's hand. "That was no excuse, but thank you for understanding."

"So how did things go after we talked?"

Darla reclaimed her tea mug and settled back to describe the events of the past days up to the point where she'd decided to come home.

Natalie listened attentively and even teared up a little when Darla recounted the sunrise boat ride. She was also just as shocked to hear about Jessica's mom as Darla and Clifton had been.

When Darla finished, Natalie said, "My goodness. You've only been gone a few weeks, but I'll bet it's felt more like months after all of that."

"It really has," Darla agreed.

"I hate to pry again, Darla, but what about Clifton?"

"What about him?"

"You said he'd decided to work on his friend's project down there, but where did that leave things between you two?"

"He asked me to stay with him while he worked on the project."

"But you didn't," Natalie observed gloomily.

Darla abruptly stood and collected their cups. "How about a refill?"

"I'm good. Thanks."

Instead of going to the kitchen, Darla set the cups down again and folded her arms. "The fact is, Natalie, I have issues. You've been around long enough to see that for yourself. I—I have a hard time letting people in. I'm afraid they'll see the messiness that *I* don't even want to face half the time, let alone inflict on someone I care about.

"Oh, I'm not trying to take the easy way out. Really, I'm not. I'm finally working on things that happened years ago, with God's help. But it won't be a simple path, and I don't want to drag Clifton along for the ride."

Natalie stood and arched her brow. "Aren't you afraid of going along for his ride too?"

Darla put her hands on her hips. "What do you mean by that?"

"I mean the man sounds like he's got some serious baggage to me," Natalie remarked with the tiniest hint of a sneer.

"Don't say that!" Darla felt her blood pressure rise.

Natalie shrugged elaborately. "I don't mean it wrong, but he does. All that loss and pain: it does things to a person's head. No wonder he's afraid of commitment, like you said."

"No! I was wrong about him. I told you that—"

"I don't blame you for being cautious," Natalie continued as if she hadn't heard Darla's outburst. "You don't want to be saddled with his problems too."

"Natalie, stop! That's not why I'm cautious. I don't care how much he's been through or how long it takes. I'd consider it an honor to walk beside him through it." Her voice went watery. "H-he's worth it." She sat down shakily. "He's worth it."

Several beats of silence passed until a steady hand fell on her arm. She looked up at Natalie to see all trace of cynicism gone from her friend's face. She'd only contrived it temporarily, of course. *Such an actress.* "He's worth it, you say?"

Darla nodded once.

"So. Are. You." Natalie's gaze was kind but intent as she sat down beside Darla. "Yes, I *am* new to faith and God's ways and everything. And in the past, I used up way more than my fair share of chances. Yet God loved me enough to give me another one.

"You are part of the reason I know about that love, Darla. I simply can't believe that your chance isn't out there waiting for you too, if you'll have the faith to reach for it."

Darla sat still, letting Natalie's fervent words wash over her. As she did, her pulse began to tap out a hopeful beat: *Reach for it. Reach for it. Reach for it.*

She leaned forward and pulled Natalie into a fierce hug. "Thank you, Natalie. What would I do without you?"

Natalie laughed on her shoulder. "I could ask you the same thing, but the more compelling question is: what are you going to do now?"

29

Clifton sat on the patio of a bustling Pensacola cafe and savored the brilliant Florida sunshine and the "oldies" playlist the restaurant piped through a speaker not far from his table. He was just about to order a second glass of sweet tea when Jessica approached.

He stood and pulled out her chair, noting that she appeared wearier than she had a few days ago but otherwise in good spirits. "Thanks for agreeing to meet me today, Jessica."

"Yeah, of course."

Once they had ordered their lunch, Jessica scooted closer to the table, her forehead puckered in a worried grimace. "I know you already said this in your email, but are you sure it was okay to send you that video clip?"

"It was more than okay. You'll never know how much it meant to me."

The tension in her face eased, and she said, "That's good. It makes me feel better to watch it sometimes."

"I can see why."

Their food arrived and, as they settled in to enjoy it, Clifton said, "How are things going with the new job?"

Jessica carefully cut her BLT halves into quarters. "I just started the training part. Then there will be a sort of probationary two weeks, but so far, it seems cool."

Cool. Not the "sooo cool" he'd expect when she was describing something she was genuinely excited about. Maybe there was an opening there.

He chewed his patty melt for a minute, then set it down and wiped his hands. "All right, here's the deal. I know you're just getting settled in and everything, but how would you feel about another job offer?"

Her eyebrows lifted. "Job offer?"

"Yeah. I will be doing some of my architecture work again. I think I'm going to keep things on a smaller scale for now, but it will be enough that I could use an assistant for some of the administrative work. Would you be interested in helping me out with that?"

The corners of her mouth lifted in an immediate smile, but she quickly sobered. "Clifton, that's really nice of you, but I'm just starting out. How do you know if I'll even be any good at it?"

"I don't, but I have my suspicions that you will be. As for starting out, well, I'll be honest with you: that's what it feels like I'm doing too. Restarting, at least. So we're in the same boat."

"Is the work going to be down here, around the Gulf?"

"The first job is. I can't be sure after that. I used to travel to do different jobs, so there might be some of that. Would that be an issue?"

"No. I don't really feel tied to this place since Mom isn't here. It just seemed like a good starting-off point."

He nodded his understanding. "Sooo, is that a 'yes' to the job?"

Jessica looked out at the cars and pedestrians passing the restaurant, seemingly deep in thought. But finally, she refocused on him. "Yes, I would like the job. Thank you."

"Good!" He reached out and shook her hand. "I'd say this has been a successful first business lunch."

They started eating again, but before long, Clifton paused. "You know? Not that I'm complaining, but I thought you'd be a little more reluctant to accept."

"Why is that?"

He shrugged. "I suppose it's because of your robust independent streak."

She took a bite of her sandwich and nodded slowly without responding.

Memories of Jessica's past conversations and behavior swarmed through his mind for a moment. Suddenly, he looked up. "No. It's not just an independent streak, is it? It's refusal to be someone's obligation again."

She swallowed noisily and stared. "How did you know?"

He chuckled at her surprise. "Believe it or not, an old dog can still figure out a trick or two now and then. Anyway, I hope your accepting the job means you know I didn't offer out of obligation."

She smiled. "Yeah, I know that. But I also realized I have to get over myself."

"What do you mean?"

"Well, it's like what I talked about with Darla a couple of times."

"Darla?" he repeated loudly enough to prompt a woman at the next table to gape at him.

Jessica frowned but continued. "Yeah. See, she says God brings people into our lives for a purpose, and sometimes that's so we can help each other. And she looks for the opportunity to help."

Clifton leaned back in his chair. His thoughts drifted back to that night Darla had knocked on his hotel room door and refused to leave until he talked to her. "That sounds like her."

"I'd like to learn to be that way too."

"It's a good aspiration, and I'd say you're well on your way."

"Thanks, but that's where I see the problem with the 'independent streak.' If you never learn how to accept help or kindness, then you may never learn how to show it either." She picked up her glass of tea and took a long drink. "I've been thinking about my aunt lately. I wonder if she's the way she is because no one ever showed her real generosity. Or maybe she wouldn't accept it if they did.

"I guess my point is I'd rather learn my lesson now. Take help when it's offered instead of pushing it away. And who knows? Maybe one day I can be the one to give it to other people. Maybe even my aunt."

"I have no doubt you will." Clifton scooted up to the table, but his attention wasn't on his food yet. If only Darla were here listening to Jessica right now. She'd be pleased. He could picture her face softening with affection as the girl spoke.

His mind began to wander. What was she doing, now that she was back in New York? Had her life returned to normal?

As if reading his thoughts, Jessica abruptly asked, "Clifton, what happened with you and Darla?" She leaned on the table. "It seemed like you guys were getting pretty tight."

Inside, he groaned a little. Wrestling up a playful scowl, he said, "Humph. That's a pretty personal question. I *am* your boss now, you know?"

Jessica's green eyes twinkled. "Oh, sorry. I meant, what happened with you and Darla, boss?"

He chuckled despite the ache winding its way through him. "A big, fat nothing is what happened." His tone held more bitterness than he'd intended. "I offered, but she turned me down."

"Offered what, exactly?"

"You know," he hedged, "a test run."

"Oh." Jessica blinked once and frowned. "How sweet."

"Okay, look," he held up his hands. "I'm sure that doesn't sound very romantic to someone your age. But when you get older like us, you tend to be a bit more cautious about things."

Her face turned grave. "Hmm," she replied, "I would think that would just make time feel more precious, especially in your case."

"Yeah, well . . ." He stopped and swallowed. He didn't really have an answer for that.

Yes, it seemed wrong to take any day for granted or to fill up time with testing out and caution and trying to decide if he was committed or not. But what else could he have done? It wasn't logical to expect Darla to leap off into a serious relationship knowing his past as she did.

And he'd been right! Darla had left.

He blew out an exasperated breath. "But Darla didn't want to take the risk. That's the main thing. How I approached her doesn't matter."

Jessica leaned on the table. "Even though you approached her like she was a long shot?"

"What?" He pushed his chair back slightly. "No! *She's* not the long shot. I am. And she knew that's what I meant." He paused. It was his turn to stare out at the traffic. "Or maybe she didn't," he muttered. "Maybe she thought *I* was the one being cautious about *her*. Like I was giving myself an out. In case I wanted to up and walk out on her one day . . ."

His gaze flew to Jessica, who sat, arms crossed, watching him try to work it out.

"Just like her fiancé did." His breath came out in a whoosh.

Jessica shrugged. "If a woman tells you what happened with her ex, she has basically given you a playbook of what *not* to do . . .

boss."

He sent her a glare. Had he really just hired this bundle of wit? In a few months, he'd probably be calling her "boss." Because she was right.

He slumped back in his chair. Jessica didn't say any more.

Traffic buzzed by. The patio speaker crackled once, then Paul McCartney's winsome vocals filtered out singing, "Hey Jude."

His thoughts drifted with the tune for a moment, then focused. Darla thought he was uncertain about her. But he wasn't.

His mouth lifted in a jaw-aching smile as he pictured her. He was absolutely certain that Darla Mayhew was infuriating, sarcastic, stubborn . . . and unbelievably compassionate and wise. And she deserved to be certain of him too.

30

Even on the most harried days of her thirty-year career in corporate Manhattan, Darla couldn't recall hustling under a greater sense of urgency than the one driving her down the quiet little bayside boardwalk.

Her footsteps clattered on the wood and her eyes scanned back and forth.

She said they would be down here.

A misty breeze wafted by, blowing bits of sand into her eyes. Impatiently, she blinked it away, and that's when she spotted them.

Just a few yards away, Clifton and Jessica sat on a bench with some wind-rustled papers between them.

Drawing closer, she could make out their conversation.

"I really have to go now, Jessica," Clifton complained with a glance at his watch. "I think you have enough to get you started." He patted the girl's shoulder, and his firm, handsome jaw softened. "You don't have to learn everything in one day, okay? You can take your time."

Kind and understanding as always. Everything inside Darla felt as radiant as the sunlight shimmering off the surrounding water.

"We'll go over it some more when we get back," Clifton concluded.

Darla stepped forward. "Going somewhere?"

Jessica glanced up first, her eyes sparkling with mischief as she regarded Darla.

Then Clifton shot to his feet and faced her. "Darla!" His blue-gray eyes were wide and questioning. "How did you know I was here?"

"Jessica," she explained.

He twisted to look at the girl, and she slid off the bench to her feet. "Okay, then. I think I'll just go take a walk and look for jellyfish or something."

Once Jessica had shuffled off, Clifton returned his attention to Darla. His face turned unusually serious. "What are you doing here, Darla?"

It wasn't the friendliest of welcomes, but it would have to do. With a halting step forward, she said, "I came to see if you're still up for that test run."

"No!" he all but shouted.

She took a small, mortified step backwards. "O-oh, I see."

He gave a sharp shake of his head. "No, I mean no test run." He closed the distance she'd just put between them. "I was about to head to New York just now to tell you I don't need a test run."

"You don't?"

His features transformed with a broad, joyous smile. "No, because my mind is made up. I love you."

She drew in a sharp breath, and everything went still.

He took one more step until they were almost touching. "You woke me up, Darla. First, with your hostility."

Humor danced in his eyes, and her cheeks heated.

"And then, with your incredible heart." Reaching up, he caressed the side of her face. "I trust that heart, and I want you to know you can trust mine."

He glanced down. "That last part might be hard. I know I'm not the best at loving people, but—"

"Yes, you are!" She finally found her voice, although it came out watery. "You've always loved. It's in everything you do. Even when you couldn't feel it, and even when you thought you were broken, you loved. That's why I *do* trust you, Clifton Peters. And it's why I love you too."

His kiss was swift and exuberant, stealing her breath with its suddenness.

When they finally broke apart, Clifton grinned and pressed his forehead to hers. "I have two questions for you."

She stole another quick kiss. "Okay, shoot."

"First off, will you marry me?"

Caught off guard, she pulled back. "Really?"

He gave a confident nod. "Really. After the job here, we can travel and keep a home base in Texas or New York, if you'd like. Or we can stay put. We can work out the details of where we go later, just as long as we go together."

"That sounds like quite a few details, but okay."

He rolled his eyes. "Well, sure, there are several details but—wait, did you say 'okay'?"

"I did. That was a 'yes,' in case you were wondering."

His grin returned in full force.

"What was the second question?" she asked.

"The second question is about staying here until I'm finished. Would you be okay with that, or do you still think being by the water is touristy and overrated?"

She pretended to glower at his teasing, but she knew it was unconvincing. "No, I don't think that anymore."

"What do you think, then?"

Her gaze traveled from him to the water, to the wide-open sky and settled on Jessica, who was standing farther down the boardwalk, unsuccessfully acting like she wasn't watching them.

Returning her focus to Clifton, Darla said, "Right now, I think it's exactly where we belong."

The End

THANK YOU!

Dear reader

I hope you enjoyed Darla and Clifton's story, and that it encouraged you in your own personal walk with the Lord. You'll find further inspiration and encouragement on The Potter's House Books Website, (www.pottershousebooks.com) and by reading the other books in the series. Read them all and be encouraged and uplifted!

Find all the books on Amazon and on The Potter's House Books website.

If you enjoyed *Where Do They All Belong*, please consider leaving a review on Amazon or Goodreads.

I'd also love to connect on Facebook, Twitter, or BookBub. Also, don't forget to check out my author newsletter, where I talk about my books and the books and authors I admire.

Blessings!
Chloe

ACKNOWLEDGMENTS

It is an honor and blessing to be one of the Potter's House Series 2 authors. I'm so grateful for my fellow PH2 authors and for Becky, our virtual assistant extraordinaire. I want to thank Marion for the cover design and Tracy Donley for the excellent editing work.

I'm also thankful for my family, brothers and sisters in Christ, and friends who have given me so much love and support as I was writing this. In addition, I owe a giant THANKS! to early readers Valerie, Wendy, Paula, Andi, Cyndi, Kimberly, Karen, and Donna. Thank you for your time, corrections, feedback, and, most importantly, for your transparency in sharing how this story connected with you. I also want to thank my amazing early reviewer friends for all the enthusiasm and encouragement.

Thank you, fellow author Sharon K. Connell, for helping me come up with "Jess's Heart Songs" for the name of Jessica's fictional YouTube channel and author friend Candace West for synopsis help. I also owe a debt of gratitude to Rick Johnson, curator of the Briarwood Nature Preserve in Saline, LA for the gracious assistance with my research.

Most importantly, I thank the Creator of all things who shares the Creative Spirit with each of us. May your love always inspire the stories we tell one another.

ABOUT THE AUTHOR

Chloe S. Flanagan is an author, technical writer, blogger, and graduate of New York University. She enjoys exploring the Christian walk frankly and thoughtfully in her fiction and in her blog, The Candid Corinthian. When she's not writing, Chloe loves music, travel, reading books in all genres, and spending time with family.

Other books by Chloe S. Flanagan:

An Offer of Grace: A Christian Romantic Suspense Series

Forward to What Lies Ahead

A Time for Every Matter

No Longer a Stranger